True Colours

MICHAEL SAGAR-FENTON

ISBN **978 185022 215 6**

Published by Truran, Croft Prince, Mount Hawke,
Truro, Cornwall TR4 8EE
www.truranbooks.co.uk

Truran is an imprint of Truran Books Ltd

Printed and bound in Cornwall by R. Booth Ltd,
Antron Hill, Mabe, Penryn, TR10 9HH

1

Simon stood in the hall, with a cream envelope in his hand.

His eyes had opened just a few moments before to a cold winter's morning. He breathed deeply in and out several times, his breath hanging in the air. The chill of the hall floor seeped into his bare feet. Simon didn't usually care about the post, but the snap of the letterbox had cut through a sequence of disturbing dreams, bringing him awake in a sweat of relief. Bills, junk, and a cream envelope.

He wandered into the kitchen and reached automatically for the kettle. Outside the window the gulls were sitting silently on roofs of slate. The town was hibernating. He switched on the radio for a human sound, though he didn't listen to the words. In the bathroom he looked at his own reflection. Fair hair, stubble, well-shaped face, brown eyes, expressive mouth. All secrets tucked away. It always pleased Simon to see how few tracks life had left on his face.

The envelope was on the table. Playing games with his own curiosity he left it there and threw some bread into the toaster. He looked out of the window for a moment, stretched his arms up to the ceiling, yawned, then sat down. Taking the paper knife Grace had given him – in full awareness that to give a knife was bad luck – he opened it.

It was typical of Andrew to write. Anyone else would have rung or emailed, but Andrew was old school and liked to do things in the proper way. It was on his professional letterhead, handwritten with a fountain pen, and couched in his usual world-weary voice:

Dear Simon,
I'm very pleased to tell you that Kurt at the Dangerfield has had a terrible bust-up with Aimee. Awful for them of course, but very good for us.

Aimee's exhibition was due around the end of May, and they aren't even talking, except through solicitors. Kurt now has a space to fill. Would we like it? I imagine we would.

Assuming the answer yes, I have already accepted on your behalf. Congratulations. I'm sure you're ready for a London outing, and I will see to it that you get the exposure you deserve. I'll be down soon to discuss the details. In the meantime you should get to work.

Please don't let this go to your head.
Yours,
Andrew Statham

Simon sat and stared out of the window. Then he read the letter again twice, before putting it down. It wasn't his style to punch the air or let out a whoop. Anyway this was too big. He looked around the empty sitting-room. That was the worst part of living alone, when something good happened and there was no-one to tell.

He imagined the reaction in the arty world which had long ago attached itself to the fishing village and holiday resort. Art was big business now, the cuckoo chick elbowing the older trades out of its way. Other artists would be nice about it, effusive, eaten up inside. But no-one would know what it really meant to him. After beating on the door for so long, one winter morning with a sweet click it opens without his help. The Dangerfield. There was of course one person who would understand too well, but it would be his pleasure not to tell her. Jane could get to hear about it in the usual way, as the gossip-mill rolled. Oh yes, did you know, Simon's got a show at the Dangerfield, I expect you probably knew already, isn't it wonderful, pity you hate each other so much. You obviously haven't screwed up his life as much as you thought.

Simon got up and dressed. He had to tell someone. Ti came to mind, since she'd always given him every chance, and her gallery was one of the few which stayed open in the winter. He checked his clothes, and combed his hair. He hurried out into the misty wind and walked quickly down towards the harbour, turning into the empty shopping street.

Ti's gallery was open, but she was not there. A stranger greeted him, looking up from her book.
    'Sorry. She's gone away for a few days.'
The girl's voice was bright and warm. He looked at her more closely. She had dark hair and eyes and an alert face, and a mouth which seemed ready to smile given an excuse. She was new to Simon. In the winter it was a small town indeed, and there were few faces which did not ring a familiar bell, especially attractive ones.
    'Can I help?'
    'Not really. Do you know when she'll be back? Where is she?'
    'Portugal. She's coming home at the weekend.'
    'Right.'
He remembered Ti's annual pilgrimage to friends in Lisbon, who did … was it stained glass? Simon looked quickly around the pictures on display, then back to the girl. 'Are you a friend of Ti's?'
    'No, I just work here. I started just after Christmas.' After a moment she continued, 'I gather it's not always this quiet.'
    'No,' Simon smiled, 'it isn't. In the summer you can't catch your breath. You don't expect much to happen this time of year. Good time to catch up with some reading.'

'Yes, we've only sold a few bits of jewellery since I started. No paintings at all. Not even any of yours.' she added.

Simon looked up sharply. Her smile really was lovely, twinkling, intelligent, with a reservoir of good humour. 'I recognised you from some of the back catalogues. I've had plenty of time to catch up.'

'What's your name?'

'Jo.'

'Please call me Simon.'

He fell suddenly silent, oddly shy, and started looking at the silver jewellery in the display case. After a pause she said, 'OK. When?'

'What?'

'When can I call you Simon? We have to be talking first.'

He gave an embarrassed laugh. 'I'm sorry.'

'How's your work going? Anything good coming up this year?'

'Well that's just it … Do you break for lunch?'

'I usually have a sandwich, but I could. I don't think I'd be seriously missed.'

'It's just that I've had some brilliant news, and I just have to tell someone.'

Jo looked grave. 'You could try your mother,' she said seriously, 'parents love to hear stuff like that.'

Simon took a deep breath 'My mother is certified, my father's dead, I never talk to my sister, I've no partner, half my best friends live miles away, Ti's in Portugal, and no-one else will care a bit. Will you please come and sit down somewhere, have a drink and look pleased for me?'

'Is it really good? It's not just a kind word in the local rag? A twenty-five pound Premium Bond? I'd hate to look disappointed.'

'Look,' he started, exasperated.

'I'm coming,' she laughed, reaching for her bag. 'You've just saved me from terminal boredom. I haven't spoken to a soul all morning. I owe you a drink for that. I don't mind how good your news is.'

'Oh yes,' said Simon, as Jo locked the gallery, 'it is.'

'I know the Dangerfield,' said Jo, drink in hand. 'I know it really well. I did a work experience there when I was in college. The other students were really jealous. The guy who ran it then was called Kurt.'

'He still is.'

'Brilliant man, absolutely crazy. He used to make us close our eyes and listen to paintings, or turn out all the lights and make us look at the collections by candlelight. Or play Blind Man's Buff with the sculptures. Actually it did wonders for our spatial awareness. I'm probably talking too much.'

'No.'

'I know I am. It's just the talk-deprivation of working where nobody goes. And I don't usually drink at lunchtime. It'll wear off. Who else can you tell? Have you got any children?'

Simon paused over his soup. 'Not really,' he said.

Jo ate as she spoke, with unselfconscious enjoyment. 'What, you haven't really got any, or you've got some but they aren't very real?'

'My ex-partner has a daughter. I helped to bring her up, and I still see her. You?'

'No. No issue. No problem. God, we haven't drunk to your show! The Dangerfield was reckoned to be pretty hot shit, if you'll pardon the expression.'

Simon nodded his forgiveness.

' ... and it was the place to be seen. Art journalists seething over it all the time. Well done!'

She raised her glass to him, eyes sparkling. Simon grinned back. This was more like it. Another half-hour passed in a moment, then Jo looked at her watch, 'I suppose I'd better get back to my public,' she said. She looked up at Simon, 'Unless you can think of something else I can use as an excuse. Some art emergency?'

'No, I suppose I'd better get on too.'

Jo looked up again, suddenly sobering. So that was that. Pity. Lunchtime drinking always had a shocking effect on her libido, and for a moment she had been toying with the idea of continuing the afternoon back at her cottage. But the note of caution in his voice banished any such visions.

'I suppose you're busy too. Really busy I mean.'

'Yes, yes I am,' Simon said. He'd withdrawn completely. She stood up.

'Thanks for the drink.'

'I enjoyed it. Can we do it again?'

'Yes. When?'

'I'll ring you at the gallery.'

And he walked slowly up the centre of the empty street alone, like a cat.

He didn't ring the next day, or for several days after. It gave Jo time to sound out other opinions of him. Most of the other artists gave him grudging respect because his paintings sold. She learned all about his long relationship with Jane. They had been the golden couple of the artists' community for years, a fixture on the scene. People had been amazed when they had finally split after so many false alarms. Jane was variously reckoned to be passionate, warm, funny, irascible and impossible. Simon was liked, but without much warmth, reputedly cool and difficult to know. Ti thought he was sweet but spoilt. The gays all thought him beautiful but not worth the trouble.

Then one evening, as she locked up, he was leaning against the shop next door waiting for her. He asked her if she had any plans for supper.

'Sorry, I'm busy tonight.'

'Anything you can put off?'

She looked at him carefully. He was real to her now, someone with a history and a context. He was lean and attractive and dressed well, but Ti was right. He was spoilt. Anyone who tangled with him could only be a rival to himself.

'Sorry. You were going to ring.'

'I meant to. But I'm not very good at that sort of thing. Never was.'

'It's quite easy. You dial numbers and say stuff.'

'I mean … I'm out of practice. Come to supper.'

His eyes were intense and moist. Bored as she was with her own company, she decided on a higher risk strategy.

'No. Ring me tomorrow and do it properly. Good night, Simon.' And she turned and walked briskly off to the car park.

He did. The invitation was formal, and the supper was probably pricier than the one he had had in mind the night before. The wine was particularly good, and Simon was lively and amusing. They wandered back to his flat automatically, as if they had made the journey together many times before.

In the bathroom Jo had a cold moment of panic. It was too easy. She was too easy. Half the point of fleeing from London had been to become a temporary nun, to live with herself on her own terms, single, independent. It had worked too. For months she had set her own schedules, eating what she pleased, waking, sleeping, going and coming without negotiation or reference to anyone's wants. She lived untroubled by quarrels or mealtimes or someone else's socks … She checked herself with a grin. Simon was an attractive one night stand, no more or less, and here she was thinking about socks. Blowing herself a kiss she walked out of the bathroom in Simon's robe and turned off the light.

2

'So what brought you here, so far from civilisation?' Jo asked happily in the darkness.

'It's different for artists.'

'Of course,' she said with exaggerated respect.

'No, I didn't mean to sound pompous. It's the end of the world for anything else, but it's not a bad place for an artist to be. If you get a reputation here, it's better than being part of the ant hill in London or somewhere.'

'Oh. I thought it was all to do with inspiration from the landscape.'

'Christ no. At least I don't think so.'

'That's not what it says on your exhibition literature.'

'No. I know. But what can you say?'

They fell silent for a moment, trying half-heartedly to think of suitable words. She half turned to look at his profile in the faint light from the harbour. She had forgotten how difficult it was meeting people in bed. So near, and so far.

'Seizing his inspiration from the elemental far west of Cornwall, where the lost land of Lyonesse still haunts the sunset as it lays its blood-red path across the water ...'

He was quiet for a while, and she wondered belatedly whether his sense of humour allowed for satire, especially of his creative sources. But he was up with her:

'Dazzled by the luminescence of the sea light and the majesty of the ancient granite headlands ...'

'Tuning in to the Celtic dreamscape ...'

'Seduced by bullshit and money. Let's talk about something else.'

But already her thigh was climbing smoothly over his, her hair was in his face, and they did not talk again until morning.

Simon was up early, making tea and small talk. Jo put on a T-shirt and stumbled sleepily around the flat. It was small but made spacious and bright by a wide view across the harbour. The clouds reflected in the water, and the few boats which braved the winter moorings were brightly coloured, rocking and pulling on their ropes like horses ready to run. It was beautiful, never still. Simon lived neatly, which was unnerving, but there were a few shelves of books, and of course paintings everywhere. Simon was receding once more into himself, prior to easing her out. She recognised the signs, but this time she was ready.

'Do you have to work this morning?' she asked brightly.

'Yes. I teach part-time and I have a class this morning.'

'Shame. I should be going too.'

The sun broke through the clouds and picked out the lichen-covered stones of the harbour wall. A flock of birds was sitting in the water, washing and chattering.

'But I'm not.'

Simon looked up, startled. 'Not what?'

'Not going. I'm going to stay here and make love to you again instead.'

'I really can't.'

'Ring in sick.'

'I couldn't.'

'I'm going to.' She paused, assessing her next move. 'Anyway you're not really a teacher. You're an artist, and artists should do what they feel.'

'It's not that simple – Jo, stop it, I can't.'

'You really have got lovely hands, Simon.'

Simon tried once more. 'Jo, I …'

'Just let it happen …'

His eyes fluttered and closed. They both rang in sick.

'You don't keep any family photos do you?'

Jo was wandering around the flat at lunchtime, feeling idle and nosey.

'No thanks,' said Simon. 'Do you?'

'Yeah. My mum, dad, sister's wedding. Stuff like that.'

'I've told you what my family are like. It would be a chamber of horrors.' She laughed.

'I've got some in a box somewhere if you really want to see The Brigadier on parade. My mother trying to remember how to smile. My sister trying not to smile. None of them seem to be related to me. They're like a …' he stopped for a moment , looking for the simile, 'Like a Film Club film. In black and white.'

'Oh, arty. Sub-titles?'

'Definitely. But in a language I never understood.'

A couple of days later Simon's head appeared unexpectedly around the door of Ti's gallery.

'There's a party tonight. Want to come?'

Childishly Jo bit her lip and played for time. Here we go.

'Do you want me to come?'

'Why not?'

'Because we'll be seen together, Simon. Something quite different from the naughty little private affair we're having now. Up a level. Closer to the scent of commitment you find so scary.'

'Yeah then.'

'Good.'

The head disappeared.

The party was held in a spectacularly messy flat right on the edge of the beach. Gelda was believed to be Finnish and worked in beaten copper, always clad in dirty overalls over her strong beefy shoulders. Whenever she had finished a large piece of work she liked to fill her flat with people to celebrate. Her own drinking powers were legendary even in a town famous for its consumption.

Everyone knew Simon. He was attentive and introduced Jo to more people than she could possibly remember. Some of them were gallery regulars. Some knew her from Ti's gallery, even remembered her former artless lines of questioning about Simon and smiled in a conspiratorial way to see her at his side. Others simply paused briefly as they took in the new shift in the local landscape. But no-one said anything to the point.

Late in the evening she heard a new voice cutting across the crowd, 'Danny, you've been plucking your eyebrows again. It leaves a scar you know … Howard can you grab me some white …'
Simon tensed visibly. Soon a striking woman surged through the crowd, followed by an older man. Jo didn't need to be told who she was. Jane was tall and looked like a mature lioness, with wild tawny hair and beautiful teeth. Her face was mobile and vivacious, challenging and confident. She wore a lacy black top which was much too young for her, but which she carried off with easy bravado. Her deep musical voice grew louder with alcohol, and her intimidating stare could suddenly break up into uninhibited laughter.

No-one knew where they were with Jane, which was how she liked it. Howard, her companion, was older, with fine features which had melted under the burden of alcohol, not a modern gay but a true homosexual of the old school, a touch of Noel Coward, always ready to amuse. Jane caught sight of Simon across the crowded studio, and her eyes lit up. As she closed on him Jo took a sudden interest in a large seascape beside her.

'Simon, darling!' Jane boomed. 'Nice to see you've started patronising Gelda the Welder again. Have you got over me at last?

Howard! Simon's here. He's come out, so to speak.'

Her gaze swept over Jo just once, like a brightly malevolent lighthouse. Simon did not introduce them, and Jane took full advantage by staying for an excessively long time, engaging in shrill small talk, and never again noticing Jo who was standing right beside her.

They went home in silence. Simon eventually broke it.
    'I'm sorry,' he said. 'I couldn't bear to let her get her teeth into you.'
    'I'm tougher than I look. Arty types don't scare me.'
    'Yes, but she's really vicious. She's good at it. I couldn't have stood by and watched.'
    'Were you really in love with her?'
    'Oh yes. I was. She wasn't always so gross.'
    'I just can't imagine you two together.'
    'No. Me neither.'
Her hand sought his as they walked silently to the flat.

    'I'm not really getting the picture' said Nadia, on the phone. 'How often do you see him?'
    'When we like. Not all the time.'
    'When who likes?' Nadia pressed.
Jo paused. Nadia had appointed herself Jo's protector since primary school, always ready to despair aloud at her weakness, compliance, lack of ambition, and willingness to be led, especially by men. She had already read Jo's pause, 'When he likes, I'm thinking.'
    'Mostly, yes. But I don't mind that, really I don't. I didn't come down here for romance.'
    'No. You were set on getting your leg over some huge stinky Cornish fisherman, if I remember rightly. What went wrong with that?'
    'Wait 'til you see them.'
    'I won't get worked up. But watch it with Simon, yeah? I know

what you're like.'

Yes, thought Jo after she put down the phone. Everybody knows know what I'm like. The memory of Steven filled the room, and she sighed as his ghost arose. Her enduring vision of Steven was his back view, silhouetted against the glare of a computer. He was a writer, so-called, tangled in a novel which wouldn't come out. She found this romantic at first, pouring all her efforts into supporting his quest. She earned their money, cooked their meals, washed and cleaned, spent long evenings on her own. Cheered him up too, at first. It all served, as Nadia said, to polish the chip on his shoulder to a nice sharp edge. He made her feel ordinary and small. She had no creative ambitions of her own and was in awe of those who had. He knew that, and never hesitated to confront her with it.

In the end the claustrophobia of living with him came to a head. Her submissiveness exploded in rages of resentment, while he stared at her in amazement and contempt. She packed, in angry tears at the wasted time and effort, crashing the door behind her with dramatic pleasure. She took a taxi to Paddington and caught the first train to Cornwall to her uncle's cottage up in the moors. It was supposed to be a short break, but she revelled in the space and quiet.

Occasionally she would turn up something in the cottage which reminded her of Steven, a book, a scarf, a CD he liked, and rage at herself all over again. Simon was not unlike Steven, she thought, in his serious self-absorption, but he didn't hate other artists for their success the way Steven hated other writers. In Steven's world no-one made it to the top except via lucky connections or actual bribery. Simon didn't seem to feel threatened by other painters at all. He walked Jo through the contemporary scene with an insider's knowledge, showing a feminine enjoyment of gossip, but no real malice. In many other ways too he was a breath of fresh air. Their relationship was casual and easy. They never quarrelled or asked personal questions about each other's doings during their frequent separations. Jo did not even know Simon had been to Italy for a week until he came back. Sometimes, Simon said, he just liked to drop off the radar. It was civil and undemanding.

But that too was the worm in her apple. In addition to their nifty sex lives, she was beginning to like him. Despite his selfishness, she was beginning to miss him when they didn't meet. Being grown-up was fine, but after a while it was too bloodless, too orderly, too many of the qualities she had left London to escape. Nadia would say that it was going nowhere, drifting, that she was just a convenience. Nadia hadn't actually said any of those things, but Jo filled in her pauses for her, argued with herself, tried not to mind, resolved to enjoy it while it lasted, make the best of it, and every other cliche from the problem pages. It wasn't a problem. Until it suddenly became one.

3

They had kissed warmly and tenderly when he arrived at the cottage. She poured him a drink. They talked while she made dinner. Simon was happy, his work was going well. A few lines about his paintings had turned up in 'Country Life'. It was nothing major, none of it, which is why it was nice. Dinner was ready. Coffee, contented sighs, a glass of brandy. Another kiss …

Jo had what her friends called a 'blurting gene'. Simon looked lazily at her over the candles, eyes dopey with food and lust. He had caught the first sun of spring, his light hair blonding, his face brown, his smile white.

'I have to tell you something, but don't take it too seriously.'
His smile broadened at her earnestness. 'What?'
'I'm pregnant.'
Simon's smile froze.
'You're joking.'
'No. I'm quite sure.'
He still smiled, and made a 'whoooah' noise, as if Jo had made an unexpectedly shrewd move on a chessboard. 'Hey. Wow.' Then his mind caught up, and he stopped smiling. 'How? When?'
'It must have been that night on the beach. You remember?'

It had been an unseasonably warm night. They had parked the car under the moon and walked barefoot down the sandy path. They undressed coyly by the rocks, and Jo swam naked at night for the first time, surprised at the velvety touch of the dark water, feeling deliciously free in the blackness. They came back onto the sand, shivering, towelled each other, and held on for warmth. She could taste the salt on his skin. She lay back on the blanket, her skin still chilled even while his heat spread through her, slowly falling into the brilliance of the stars above him. It was as beautiful a way to conceive a child as one could imagine. She smiled at the memory.

Simon was not smiling. 'You should have said.'

'You should have asked.'

'It was really irresponsible. We're not kids.'

'Simon, it's done. We have to decide what to do next.'

Simon turned to face her more fully. His eyes searched for secret meanings. 'What do you mean?'

There was a growing panic there. It would be nice to play happy families just for a while before turning to practicalities, but Simon was already tossing in deep water.

'What to do. We both have to decide.'

His eyes were flicking. He needed her to let him off the hook, quickly before its barb sunk all the way in.

'Decide?'

He was desperate to be released. She could not bear to do it.

'Yes,' she said calmly, 'there's more than one choice.'

'There isn't!' He said it with a low scornful growl.

For the first time anger flashed through Jo. She realised that this was already the end. Simon was furious, betrayed, he wanted the words unsaid, deleted and gone, and himself gone after them. He was walking mindlessly up and down the cottage.

'Don't worry,' she said coldly, 'I'm not trying to make you feel trapped. I just thought you ought to ...'

'Trapped!' he said, a tone higher than before. 'I don't feel trapped. We had sex, that was all. I certainly don't want a baby, and I'm sure you don't. We'll just have to ... sort it out.'

'How do you know what I want?'

'For Christ's sake Jo ...'

'Like you said I'm not a child any more. Maybe it is time I had a kid.'

Simon was colouring, a dash of rusty pink on his cheeks. She recognised the body language. It was the same as her three-year-old nephew's, moments before a major tantrum broke. She relented.

'Simon, wake up, I don't want a baby! Why would I?'
But his blood was up.

'Now you're playing games. You are pregnant I suppose?' She nodded, suddenly all fight gone out of her. 'Perhaps you'll have it. And perhaps you won't. What about me!'

'Simon ...'

'It's the last thing I need. Christ. Do you know what I've got on at the moment? I'm just getting somewhere. In London. And now you want to ruin it.'

Jo began to tune out the words, but listened to the sound rolling around the quiet cottage as Simon bellowed with frustration. Finally he paused.

'Simon, have some coffee and calm down.'

'I'm perfectly calm,' he roared. 'I'm fine. Thank you so much for dinner. Good night.'
The door slammed hard behind him, leaving a terrible silence. She could hear his footsteps stumping down the gravel. She listened for his car, but there was no further sound.

Simon strode without seeing, following the lane and turning off onto a path across the moor. He picked up a stick and beat the gorse bushes with it as he passed, turning the tender top leaves to pulp. It was a calm night, a moist Cornish spring night full of stars, undimmed by the glow of street lights. In the distance a lighthouse swept the sea. Through his whirling senses he heard a sound behind him, and cursed to see that the little terrier Jo was minding had followed him, enthusiastically keeping up on an unexpected walk. He would keep walking until he felt better, then get in the car and leave it all behind. Jo was fresh and lovely but he was not planning on staying. He was a prisoner, recently released, not going back, not for any reason. Especially not for a child. Grace had been enough. Perhaps, yes maybe, one day, when he was at the top of his tree and ready to slow down. But that could still be years away.

He reached a stile to an open field and stopped for breath. There was no sound. A red light drew a line across the distant bay as a fishing boat made its way home. He stood with one foot up on the granite stile while the cool air calmed him. He had walked his temper out for the time being. He turned back.

When he was nearly back at the lane the dog gave a bark and disappeared into a thicket, snuffling and yelping. He called to it, quietly and then louder. He listened, but there was no sound. He whistled, but there was no response. He went towards the thicket, beating brambles aside with the stick. He felt the stick hit something harder, and bent down to look. It was a rusty strand of barbed wire.

Anxiety spread through him. He recognised the thicket for what it was, not a natural growth but an enclosed circle, guarded by wire, in which there would have been an old mine shaft. The moors had once been full of them although most had been capped or filled in. But there were still some inaccessible places where the granite shafts opened all the way down to the hidden tin mines, with only an old fence and a hedge of bramble and gorse to protect them. Sometimes dogs fell down them and had to be rescued. He split the night with whistles, but the dog had disappeared. Simon put a cautious leg over the wire.

The glow in the fireplace had diminished, but Jo was still staring. She had not moved since Simon's florid exit. She shivered, and got up stiffly. She turned on the radio, went to the toilet, put on the kettle. She was dry-eyed and in control. The deed had been done. Of course Simon would blow up like a rash – she had seen enough of him to know the suddenness of his moods, and his reactions to a situation he could not handle. All she wanted was for him to come back and talk. She waited with a head full of words, but time went on and all was quiet. Suddenly a small white shadow passed the french window. She opened it, and the little dog trotted inside, curling up at once in front of the fire. Jo went out into the garden and called Simon's name once or twice, self-consciously. Then she came back in and stretched out on the sofa again to wait, and think.

'Slip?' called Simon, 'Come on, come out.' He had heard no sound for a while and was fearing the worst. He was into the outer undergrowth and had to step over a low wall. He pulled out his torch, but the tangle was so thick he could not see the ground. He pushed gingerly forward, using his stick to test the ground ahead. He heard the bell of the church clock chime once across the fields. Then the ground suddenly lurched.

Simon stood still, not able to jump, not knowing which way was safe. His free hand gripped a gorse bush and he gasped with pain, but did not let go. He tapped gently with the stick, but the years of leaf mould absorbed the blow and gave no clue what was beneath. Slowly he shifted his weight so that he could turn round. There was a terrible soft cracking, and whatever he was standing on tilted backwards. He could hear debris falling below. Suddenly sweating, his hand slipped up the bush, its new spring spines digging deeply into the flesh between his fingers. There was another crack, another small lurch, and then the ground fell completely away. Dropping, Simon lost his hold of the bush, and his flailing arms encountered nothing but the soft ends of rotten wood and the brittle edges of ancient corrugated iron. For a moment he caught and swung on his elbows, and then his arms were up and he was free-falling through dusty root-ends into nothing. He gave a roar of fright.

4

The water saved Simon's bones, breaking his fall. It was freezing cold and made him gasp, taking it into his lungs. He coughed and struggled in the darkness, mindless and animal. His hand touched a soft muddy floor underwater and he scrabbled at it. His other hand touched, and then his knees, taking his weight. He crawled up the slow gradient and left the water behind. He panted lungfulls of clammy air, lying saturated on the muddy slope. As shivers of coldness and shock chased through him, he pulled himself further upright until his head touched something solid. Reaching up he could feel the shape of a concave roof, clay and small crumbly stones. Even through his panic came the realisation that the floor he was lying on was probably the result of a roof fall. He stopped touching the roof.

He had never known such cold. His wet jacket and jeans clung to him as if to suck his life away. He panted more regularly now, and his teeth chattered until he thought they would splinter. All around him was darkness, so profound it seemed more a presence of darkness than an absence of light. His mind raced without information, trying to find some foundation for his continuing reality, the cold, the darkness, the knowing he was not dreaming.

Jo's eyes snapped open. She hadn't meant to go to sleep. She hobbled to the window to see if the car was still there. It was. Then she rang his flat, but left no message on his answering machine.

Who to call next? Who'd like to share the excitement of a late-night domestic dispute? The neighbours? The police? Wouldn't that be great, when Simon came shambling back in at dawn after spending the night in some barn, to find the police and half the neighbourhood sitting round the living room with his pregnant girlfriend to cheer him in. There was no procedure to follow when someone disappears in the night, just one decision to make. When do you panic? She made some coffee and turned on the TV in the middle of a film.

Simon tried to find his voice: 'Help ...' It was smothered by shivers. He tried again, and the sound of his own voice brought back some sanity. Slowly he pieced the facts back together, in reverse order, from falling to searching for the dog – was the dog down here beside him? – from his anger, to Jo. And her words, which had started everything. He tried once again to call out, the sound bursting from him without power. What was the point? He was sure his voice wouldn't reach the top of the shaft. He couldn't decide how deep it was, how far he had fallen, even what damage he had suffered. He was too cold and rigid to take an inventory yet. Was it still night? If so no-one would be around to hear him, except perhaps some old drunk on his way home. And he'd be more likely to run away than to answer voices coming out of gorse bushes in the dark.

He craved light. He could not see where the water began or how far it stretched. He heard little after-falls and splashes in the pool, but could not imagine what kind of chamber he was in, how broad, what shape. He was desperate to move and stretched out one leg after the other. His left hurt a great deal, but he could move. He raised himself to a crouch, which made him cough. He moved a little way down the slope and stretched up again, finding with huge relief that he could stand. But one more step took him back into the water.

'If you wish to report a crime, press 1. If you wish to hear progress on a crime which has already been reported, press 2.'

Jo put the phone down. She could not make herself ring the police. She didn't want a real life man in uniform asking questions. She just wanted someone else to tell her what to do. She thought for a desperate second of calling her mother. Then she could let herself go and rant on for a while about Simon, his temper and his talent for taking offence and his lack of support and his arrogance and his bloody jackets. She swore out loud, making the dog jump in its sleep. She wanted a shower, and went upstairs, but came straight back down again. What if the phone rang?

Simon's mobile was dead but his watch had survived the fall, and was luminous. He stared at it hungrily. He gave himself little disciplined tasks, strictly timed. Every five minutes he changed his position and stretched. Every ten minutes he called out. In between he kept his arms moving as often as possible. It worked. Apart from one moment of blank terror when what he assumed was a toad crawled across his bare foot and jumped into the water, time went evenly. He breathed deliberately and slowly. The cold had reached equilibrium and would get no worse. It wouldn't kill him.

At twenty past seven, he noticed details emerging from the blackness. Light was filtering down the chimney he had made. He could make out the darker blackness of the water, and the dome-shape over his head. Then the further bank of the pool became visible, another beach which disappeared back into the blackness. There were a few pieces of fallen timber there, and a bundle of rubbish.

The light waxed to a faint gloom and he could see the sides of the shaft above. The sides were the same mixture of clay and pebbles. It was too wide and crumbly to climb. He could not see the top, but reasoned that it could not be too far or he would have died in the fall. There was no point in wasting his voice too much yet. His clothes had dried to a clinging damp by his body heat. He'd be alright.

Seven twenty-five.

How could Jo get pregnant? Why did she even bother to tell him? She was an independent woman with her own life. And he wasn't nearly ready to take on a full-time lover again, let alone a child. No no no. He moved his feet gingerly. Once was enough. Grace had always looked right through him as if she knew his every device, even as a small child. Maybe it was different if you were the real father, but maybe not. He wouldn't put in for more years of those accusing eyes. There were enough kids in the world already.

Although none were his. The nearest to that had been a girlfriend at art school who once missed a period. He moved again, wincing with pain. There was damage there, and a bleeding hand, and a cut on the head. Lucky really. It had finished things with the girlfriend. In the end they were too tense to talk, and could only sit exchanging resentful glances. The awfulness of it filled his days. Suddenly the world seemed full of pregnant women, tottering absurdly wherever he looked. And babies everywhere. On slings, on backpacks, and car-seats, pushchairs, in restaurants, trains, everywhere, like a bad dream. He even found himself drawing them, doodling them on old sketchpads and envelopes before throwing them furiously away. And then one day her period started, and life went on. They parted thankfully, almost without another word.

The light grew stronger. The bundle of rubbish on the other bank reminded him of a baby; if that bit was an arm, that the head, and the body tilting that way towards the water ... He snapped out of it. No more nightmares.

Birdsong came faintly down the shaft, which lifted his spirits. He crouched down for a change. He let his eyes rove around his dungeon again. In the opposite corner the walls disappeared into darkness. That must have been the way into the mine, although it seemed to be blocked. Once again Simon recalled what he could about tin mines. The shaft above may have been just an air vent. The whole of these workings were probably just an adit, a tunnel to let water drain out. If he had fallen into the deeper ore-digging workings, he would never have survived.

Again, for want of something better to look at, the bundle drew his eyes. There really was something childlike about it. The large curve which could be a head, one arm bent with a hand up to the face as if to block out the world. On an impulse he suddenly put his good hand into the cold water and threw a little spray across at it. It was hard to get the range, but at last a solid gout of water hit the target. Orange mud ran down. A deep grunting gasp forced itself from him and echoed around the chamber.

'Oh Jesus Christ,' he said aloud.

Now white and clear, the fleshless fingers, the wise domed forehead and lightly stitched fontanelles, the sightless eye sockets, toothless mouth in a clean oval of surprise, neck disappearing into the rags of a reddish garment. Something shone yellow beside it, and Simon sent another wave of spray over. It was plastic, perhaps a rattle, with a caricature of a face on it, its wide red smile still encouraging mirth and joy.

He started shouting wildly, all control gone. For some time he did not hear the distant sound of barking, or the voice that called back down to him.

5

After a while he realised that Jo's voice had stopped calling. He had not been able to make out anything she had said. Simon tried not to look at the thing opposite him. Light was pouring down the shaft, diffuse but adequate. Once or twice he even dozed in a crouching position. But when he woke it was still there.

Suddenly there was the confident sound of a man's voice. Simon's thoughts started to arrange themselves in order for the first time. 'Artist in Mineshaft Fall after Row with Pregnant Girlfriend'. There was all that to face. And even better, the 'Mystery Child' story. That really would take off, and the story would go on running. The thing on the mud must have had a mother once. How someone could have cast it into the blackness of the earth was beyond him, but there must have been a dreadful moment of decision. It was against all nature. How long had it been there? The flesh had disappeared but the clothes were still almost whole, and looked modern enough. This was a big-scale horror story. The press would not rest until the desperate woman was hunted down and her life story put on display. He stared at it again, at its face. It seemed to stare back. Innocent, but with a knowledge of its own betrayal.

'Help,' said its naked mouth. 'Help me.'

'Hello below. Can you hear me?' The man's voice boomed from somewhere above.

He didn't want this man to find it, to pick it up. To deliver it to the police, who would open a file, make forensic investigations, and keep it in evidence. Start the ball rolling. He shuddered. This wasn't a case, it was a tragedy. Something private. He couldn't let officialdom take control, not until he had come to terms with it himself. Debris was falling and the reassuring voice was getting louder. Simon found himself picking up handfuls of sticky mud and hurling them across the pool. It was hard work but he kept at it until the ivory features disappeared again, and the toy lost its bright colours.

It went dark, and more material splashed into the water. Bright, muddy boots appeared in Simon's line of vision. The man was talking on a headset. His yellow helmet came into view, and his feet touched the water. He stopped descending. His eye caught Simon's, and smiled with relief and encouragement. Simon's own eyes widened as the man landed on the opposite bank, his feet inches from the muddy bundle.

'Hello. Are you hurt?'
'Nothing much. Could do with a brandy. D-d-don't suppose you've got one s-s-strapped under your chin?' His teeth were chattering again. The man reported the latest intelligence into his microphone.
'Sorry, no brandy. But I brought you a spare one of these.' He brandished another yellow helmet. As if in a pantomime his feet suddenly left the ground without effort, and he swung over the pool, landing at Simon's side. Simon smiled but did not try further speech while the fireman secured his helmet and a safety harness.

It was painfully uncomfortable. He was slowly hauled up, his body amazingly stiff and his fingers without feeling, far colder than he had realised. Near the top he heard a voice saying 'Here he comes!' and then his head was out in the air; a second birth.

The thicket had almost all gone, cut down or flattened. Behind the safety tape a small group of onlookers were gathered, mostly strangers for all he could tell through his watering eyes. A polite cheer arose. A camera nosed towards him. He spotted Jo, between the fire engine and the ambulance which were parked, painfully bright in the morning sun, on the grassy downs. He could hardly comprehend their colours after so many hours without light. He was unhitched from the harness and remained unsteadily standing, leaning on a fireman. A paramedic came up, with Jo close behind.

'Are you alright? Are you alright?' she repeated. He gave her a tired smile.

'How did you get down there?'

'I needed somewhere quiet to sulk,' he said indistinctly, like a stage drunk. 'This man wants to examine me.'

'Am I going to hospital?' he asked the paramedic, who nodded.

'I'm going to hospital,' he said confidentially to Jo. 'Will you come and see me?'

Jo smiled, close to tears. 'Of course.'

Simon made a pretence of gathering his strength, so that he could wait and look at the face of his rescuer as he followed Simon out of the ragged hole in the ground. The fireman was empty-handed, no bundle, no ghost in his eyes. Simon relaxed and let himself be guided to the ambulance.

'Sprained left foot, bad cuts on one hand, odd cuts, big, big bruises, a touch of hypothermia. Not a bad night's work. I suppose the bloody dog's alright.' he added, remembering the purpose of his quest for the first time.

'He's fine. You were so lucky.' said Jo. She added daringly, 'Now you see what happens to men who walk out on me.'

Simon smiled below his sunken eyes. 'You said you were tough. You didn't say you had powers.'

She held his good hand tightly. The hospital was warm, a sensation so sweet he could not get enough of it. His head drooped, and then jerked upright. 'I need to sleep now.'

'I know.'

He winced as he turned over, settled heavily and then sank down through layers of comfort and pain, leaving Jo behind. She watched his eyelids twitch and jerk as his dreams began. After a while she kissed his hair and walked softly away.

There were many false starts to the next day. And then a journalist came. Simon slowly told his story while the journalist listened respectfully: the late night walk, the straying dog, the fall, the survival. The dog's redemption next morning, hearing him shouting from the bowels of the earth when Jo went out to look for him. A moral about vigilance in mining areas.

Afterwards an older nurse brought him some tea. He looked at her frankly as he'd previously looked at the cleaner, until she turned away in confused surprise. You'd be the right age. Was it yours?

Grace came.

'You're famous. You were on the lunchtime news.'

'I bet they called me a schoolteacher.'

'Ego in working order then. No, they called you a well-known local artist. Not even an idiot.'

There was always a sentinel in her face behind the banter. Her grey eyes looked concerned as she gave him a long glance. Then she relaxed.

'Anyway I'm glad you're OK. Got to get back now. I'll phone. Bye.'

She left a card on the side table.

Soon afterwards Howard entered his small world. Howard was really Jane's friend, but he had stayed close to both of them after the split. Simon found his camp bonhomie amusing and comforting as a rule. But he was tired.

'Oh dear. The English Patient. What a mess. Could you be an absolute darling and bring an old man a cup of coffee?' he continued to a passing nurse, squeezing her hand with an adoring gaze. Simon had already marked her as a dragon but, like so many others she was powerless against Howard's charm, and the coffee appeared a few minutes later. Meanwhile Howard had launched into a long story about how Verity had fallen out with Sarah at the private view of her lithographs in some dreadful gallery down a country lane where it's always foggy and full of cow shit, no, he hadn't been there himself but Neil, his current young man, had held their coats while they went at it. It became a roaring in Simon's ears but he was too feeble to protest, and knew that nothing short of a heart attack would stop him in full flight. Howard eventually turned his attention back to the bed.

'Actually, dear heart, I was amazed to find you still here. As I understand it, even if you arrive here in bits they string you back together and chuck you out before sunset.'

'They're just checking for concussion and internal injuries. I think I'm on something too – I feel woozy. Anyway I've been on the telly, so they wouldn't dare throw me out to die.'

'You don't think so?' Howard had a couple of wonderful hospital horror stories to share. Eventually he gave the dozing Simon a pat and left, greeting his nurse effusively as they passed in the corridor.

Simon was glad of the painkillers as his body woke up fully to its outrages. He could hobble to the toilet, read, or watch TV but mostly he lay and stared at nothing. He opened Grace's card. It was a standard chain store get-well, featuring a standard smiley face. He put it up by the water jug. He dozed, then woke again. The card beamed at him with its plastic smile, red and yellow beating their wings at the window of his memory. Where had he seen that smile so recently? Finally he made the connection and wearily turned it away.

6

In the evening Jo offered to take him back to the cottage. No, he said, he wanted to go back to his flat until he was better. Jo thought that was silly. Why couldn't he come back where she could keep an eye on him? He didn't know, he just didn't want to. He was petulant and childish, she was close to tears, unusually emotional. It came to him that she was still pregnant although he had already forgotten, but he was too far into the argument to retreat. He wanted to be in his own setting. He didn't want to go near Jo's place, near the broken mine, not until the ground had been made whole again and its secrets restored. But he couldn't say that. He remained obstinate, using his hurts to win the day. Jo agreed to take time off work to take him home the next day. He couldn't wait for her to leave.

None of his dreams were of the mine, but it came back every time he woke up. He tried to force himself back to sleep to dream again, through the hum and noise and interruptions of the hospital. It was a long and complex night.

After even a couple of days of institutional care, the world was a frightening, unregulated place. The traffic was loud and dirty. No-one cared if his needs were met. Jo was late. After ten minutes waiting in the windy car park, Simon sat in reception, glowering at a magazine, avoiding the eyes of the staff. He saw her coming from a long way off. A pang went through him. She was anxious and hurrying, frowning against the wind. But her long legs were eating up the car park, an unselfconscious animal stride, and her face was still beautiful and calm beneath its surface troubles. He glanced at her waist and tried to imagine it round and pregnant, her usual dash slowed to a careful tread. He shook his head. Impossible.

'Sorry,' she gasped as she burst through the automatic doors. 'Some fucking halfwit artist caught me at the door just as I was sneaking off.' He gazed at her in admiration. This wasn't going to be easy. 'How are you?' she went on. 'You look ... awful really.' She gave a nervous laugh as her words reached her own ears. 'Are you sure you're fit to go?'

'No choice. Walking wounded this way out please. Attention. Quick march. Well perhaps not.'

'OK. I've got your stuff in the car. I may have left a few things. I didn't have much time this morning. You haven't changed your mind have you?' she asked without weight, her head slightly on one side. He shook his head dumbly. 'OK,' she said, 'Let's go.'
She set off, and was out of the doors and halfway to the car before she checked and remembered the pace at which he was forced to follow. She came back with another quick laugh. 'Sorry,' she said again; too bright, too brave.

The flat was warm and felt amazingly safe. Like an animal he recognised his shape and his smell in it. They bundled the few things up the stairs. When they were all piled in the living room Simon looked with surprise. He had not realised how much his life had bled into Jo's in so short a time. Clothes, CDs, bathroom things, sketch pads. Jo put the kettle on from habit. Simon stared out of the window. The wind was drawing white lines across the dark grey water. A green trawler was leaving harbour, lowering her booms as she went, spray flicking up at her bows.

'Simon.' She was standing over him with cups of coffee. There was an uncharacteristic pause while she hunted the words. 'I know you're shaken and you've had an awful time, but – this isn't it, is it?'

He sighed. 'Sit down a minute.' She sat down slowly and looked out of the window too. But as soon as he spoke, her eyes were into his, painfully direct. 'No this isn't it,' Simon lied, slowly piecing together a speech. 'But you have to see how it is with me. First a real chance opens up for me, away from here. Then you tell me you're all-of-a-sudden pregnant, which wasn't what either of us wanted. Then I fall down a mine shaft and nearly kill myself. I'm what you might call – off-balance.'

'Of course,' she agreed quietly.

'So I just need ...'

'Some spaaaaaace ...' she said, to lighten the atmosphere.

'Yeah. Basically some space. Just for a bit. Until I know what's happened. And what it's done to me. Also I've got to get an exhibition together, with one good arm and one good leg. I'm crap to be with when I'm doing that in any case.'

'If you want to get it over,' her voice was suddenly tight, 'Now would be a good time. I'm not into relationships that die by inches. I've done that one already.'

Simon sipped his coffee. 'It's not over, Jo. I just feel like I ...' He held his fingers up against the light. 'It's difficult ... fine' he snapped, as Jo's mobile suddenly intruded with its jaunty chime.

'I'm so sorry,' she said, jumping up from the table. She took the call into the hallway and dealt with it curtly. But when she returned, Simon was standing up. She was about to apologise again, but realised from his stance that her next task was to make a civilised exit, no fuss. She kissed him on the cheek, lightly.

'I'll call you,' he said. The door closed.

In the steam of the bathroom Simon peeled off his clothes and settled painfully into the water. He gazed dispassionately at the range of colours on the skin of his legs, and thought about Grace.

Grace was not his. Jane had exploded into his life with such force that the small quiet child with the dark hair and solemn eyes seemed as natural a part of her as her huge laugh and bright clothes. Another accoutrement, the way some people own exotic pets, or in another era employed silent black servants. He had missed the earliest stages of her childhood, although he had heard no good of them. Successions of broken nights, tiredness you could taste, losing the plot about who you were and why, nappies, mucky feeding, distraction, mess. Jane had hated it all from her deepest roots. She treated Grace badly, interspersing long periods of curtness and neglect with onslaughts of wild affection. Simon tried, when he remembered, to fill the gaps. But the early part of life with Jane was full of passion, sex and rage, and he too virtually forgot about Grace for days at a time. She was often more symbol than real, a heavily loaded piece in a power game. Jane was dismissive of her, then protective, then possessive, then bored.

Grace was sixteen now, clever, sullen and sarcastic. In Simon's art classes there were many angry-faced girls like Grace, assertive and challenging, with their hair pulled sharply back from their foreheads. They were smart and self-reliant, primed to ignite without warning. 'Kids!' Jane would shout, in Grace's hearing, 'Fucking kids! Who'd have them?'

Simon glanced down at his own body. Who'd have them indeed. If they had a choice. If they only thought about it. But it was easily done. Then again his mind clouded over, and he stood up, wincing. You have them or you don't. That's the deal. You don't change your mind afterwards, and toss them into a hole in the ground.

7

Andrew Statham had a built-in sigh in his voice, due to a lifetime of dealing with artists and three decades of untipped Gauloises, which gave all his statements an air of regret. He lounged in Simon's sofa in an old green jumper, his long legs in corduroy trousers extending halfway across the carpet, ending improbably in yellow suede shoes.

'Just thought I'd better see how you are for myself,' he said, resentfully.

'Thanks,' said Simon. 'Thanks for your card too.'

"Did I send you a card? Good old Anne. I gather you're lucky to be still with us?'

'Yes. I was very lucky. I wasn't even badly hurt.' 'Well if you will live in a county full of holes like a Gruyère cheese.'

'Yes.'

There was a pause following the niceties. Andrew picked out a cigarette with long yellow fingers.

'I'm alright,' said Simon more sharply, 'I'm still on for it.'
Andrew looked at him through the flame of the cigarette lighter, which reddened his pale face.

'Are you sure?'

'I'm quite sure. I can fill the Dangerfield, no problem. With essential and saleable work.'

'I had started tentatively putting together a Plan B.'

Simon's anger started to rise. 'There's absolutely no need, Andrew. I'm perfectly alright. I've started work on it already.' It was a fat lie, but there was a lot at stake.

'I don't know,' Andrew sighed, 'I was talking to Marcus from the V & A the other day, and he thinks the Cornish thing is getting over-heated again. It's had a bloody good innings, but now every bus conductor and beach bum thinks he's an artist, and as for the galleries! More galleries than pubs now, who would ever have thought that would happen in Cornwall? And the quality ...' he said, almost to himself. 'Dear, dear,' he looked at Simon directly, 'so it did make me wonder ...'

'Wait 'til you see my new stuff,' said Simon suddenly, with unexpected confidence. 'It'll blow you away.'

'That, dear boy, is what they all say.'

'It'll blow me away too,' thought Simon, who hadn't touched a brush for weeks. 'None of us can wait to see this.'

The black and white abstract was semi-geometrical, almost retro pop art, 70cm x 50cm, on white board, local artist, price £1750. The only relieving colour was a small red dot of success in the top right hand corner. Because it was opposite her little counter, Jo had ceased to see it long ago. But in any case her eyes were on lookout duty only while her mind wandered. It was a quiet April afternoon, overcast and chilly, not the sort of weather to tempt seekers of culture out into the gusty streets. To anyone else it was a typical spring day, but for Jo it was somewhere in Week Seven, and the author of the fluttering nausea below her diaphragm hadn't rung. Or called, or even written.

She had rung him, several days running. He had been politely monosyllabic – yes he was OK, yes he was feeling better, yes he was managing alright, he was working hard, yes he would see her soon. Yes he was a perfect bastard, she thought, until reflection on the nature of bastards had changed her fury to sudden fear. No-one else knew. She had carefully negotiated phone calls home and lunches with friends, joining in the lighter gossip which she could have over-trumped with a word.

She missed Simon terribly, which made her angry with herself. She had been fine before. The cottage had given her a new life. Simon was nice looking, if self-centred, and not – she thought blasphemously – half as talented as he imagined, even if he was beginning to pull away from the pack. He thought she was attracted by his genius and charm, but her initial interest had been far more carnal. It should have stopped there. But he had grown on her, in his needy, childish way. She wanted to mother him. The classic trap. And now she was lining up to mother his offspring too.

Or, of course, not.

Loud voices brought her to earth suddenly, especially as the loudest was undoubtedly Jane's. Jo tensed up all over, and felt sicker than before. As she had expected, Jane irrupted and walked her London friends around two sides of the gallery making loud and disparaging comments about the work on display before noticing Jo, although she knew perfectly well that Jo worked there.

'Ah,' she said at last, anticipating pleasure, 'Jo, isn't it. How lovely. This is Alicia and Frank, just down for a few days, searching in vain for the new Cornish wave. *The Nouvelle Vague.*'

'Perhaps they should try the beach?' said Jo, cringing at her own awfulness. The visitors smiled palely, while Jane gathered herself, much as a real wave does before it slaps the rock.

'And how is poor Simon? Brave soldier, like daddy? Had you running with the broth and the bedpans? He always was such a baby.' She turned to her London friends, who smiled on uncomprehendingly at this confidence.

'All friends again?' she boomed on.

'We're fine thanks.' Even to her own ears it sounded flat.

'Good. No frost nipping at the darling buds, then. I so hope not. You seem made for each other.'

Two wastes of space together. Yes, we get it, you bitch, even Alicia and Frank have cottoned on. But Jane had tired of baiting her for the moment.

'Doing quite well I see.' She swept a handfull of purple nail varnish – around the walls. 'Comforting, isn't it, to see that at least the bottom always stays in the market. Just as long as it's overpriced and rubbish. No talent required. You really should move down, you know,' she said to Alicia without a pause. Jo was used to Jane's rudeness, but it still occasionally took her breath away. Alicia, however, was made of sterner stuff:

'Darling, however would I learn to be bad enough? Do you know someone who could teach me?'

They laughed together, like opera singers practising low scales. A headache added itself to Jo's discomforts. Any minute now, Jo thought, she'll notice, she'll fix me with an X-ray stare and say 'Jo, darling, aren't you looking a little pale? Not unwell I hope?' and follow it with a large wink to show that she knew that she knew that she knew.

But a pre-packed audience like Frank and Alicia proved too great a draw, and a few minutes later Jane swept them out again. As soon as her voice subsided outside Jo made a dash for the toilet, and afterwards stared at herself in the mirror. Her frightened face stared back but could offer her no comfort.

'This, class, is a piece of plain white board. Over here is a selection of paints – in this case acrylics – and in my hand is a medium size, good quality, animal-hair brush. This is what you do. You dip the brush in a colour, like so, or two or three if it takes your fancy, bear the paint to the board, here, then push, shove, wiggle and wipe until you've made a pigging mess, like … so. Then you wait for it to dry, append your name, and put it up for sale for loads of money.'

Simon paused, gazing around his empty studio in the sloping afternoon sunlight.

'Easy. Innit?'

He tossed the board onto a pile in the corner.

The studio was up a hill on the edge of the town, down a quiet lane with grassy hedges. It had been jerry-built on top of an old granite garage by one of the pre-war generation of artists who had brought the town to prominence. The garage was still below, noisy and smelly during the day, and the draughty glass panels rattled in their wooden frames, but Simon had been lucky as ever in succeeding to it in a town overcrowded with artists.

It was full of paintings, finished, half-finished, and abandoned, a china sink, all the paraphernalia of painting, and had also accumulated a fair amount of junk. Simon's neatness did not extend to his workspace. It always felt cold.

The palette which had sustained him through to his successful breakthrough had been borrowed from the coldest places on earth. He had been impressed at an early age by photographs and watercolours of Antarctica. He studied the ice caves and crevasses, blues and greens found nowhere else, sometimes back-lit by an extraordinarily cold orange. He had walked amongst the colours until he could dream in them, and learned how to translate them into forms, almost like music. Slow deep movements with heavy inner swirls in the lowest pigments, especially the big blues. Sharp staccatos of thin crystal. Grace notes of purest hurtful white. And ultimately with familiarity came cohesion, unthinking, with no need to check for harmony, and even space for adventure in the shifting curtains and continents, fissures and peaks. His best work still worked, shimmering on the naked retina in the midnight sun. He had also achieved a signature. His canvasses cut through the frivolity of the mixed show and the private view with a cool light. No-one else was exploring these frozen tones. He had what all artists craved, a voice, a style, something unmistakably his.

As he defined his work, delving deeper into the ice, he gradually realised that there were no directions back to the crossroads where all choices are equal. He painted 'his' pictures. If he tried another way, they could be anybody's. His style closed in until it rubbed against his shoulders. But success pulled him on. Why not, one more painting which would spread the word, which was what he knew people expected, which would sell? What was the point of moving sideways or down? He had ridden doggedly on his trademarks, more or less, until the ground had literally fallen from under him.

Since then nothing had gone right. Despite his reassurances to Andrew, he had no relish for painting even when he was fit enough. When he reached out for his usual marine palette, he realised that the break had fractured his flow. Like chocolates, he thought, you keep on eating them and don't realise, until you stop, how sick you feel. Then you don't want another one, ever. You want to throw them away in the corner of the studio in a big, untidy pile. Bloody blue. Grim green. The walls were covered in it, and it sang unseen from dozens of concealed racks. He was starving for the colour of ... what? Life, perhaps?

His life had been taken away and given back to him. He had come out of the cold, alive, into the warmth of colours. He still felt the shock of emerging from the frozen darkness into the sun, the colours of the sky, the garish vehicles, gorse, peoples' clothes even. Nothing in his former life shone with such warmth. Certainly nothing in the mausoleum of his work-in-progress.
Jo's hidden baby had life too, so far, if she still bore it. Even his mineshaft child, his deepest earth secret, had lived before it died, once had colours and tones, a world away from his glacial visions.

He glanced around the studio again, hungry for colour. There was nothing, except for Grace's card, which for some reason he had stuck onto a mirror. Its plastic smile caught his gaze, and held it. His other movements ceased. He became all eye, his whole being suddenly photosensitive. He remained still for a long time, full of emotions without a name, feeling the scenery within him shift. Then, with sudden purpose, he began to move.

8

It was Grace who interrupted him a long time later. The phone had rung several times before he realised, and he had to run across the studio to catch it. 'Simon!' There was a furious whine in her voice. 'Where the fuck are you? Do you know what time it is?' He knew that night had fallen, having adjusted to the change of light, but little else. 'We're playing in St Tregonnick tonight, remember. You promised to take me.'

Grace was musical, almost against her will. She could play the flute beautifully and the saxophone dirtily. She sang backing vocals in the school rock band. But she had remained strangely constant to the mediaeval harmonies of Early Music, singing a part in an ensemble in her clear, ghostly mezzo-soprano. Goth and punk, butch and tart, other phases had come and gone without shaking her involvement in the echoing layers of human sound stripped of all emotion.

'I'm on my way.'
'You'd better be. I'm practically supposed to be there by now.'

The trip passed mostly in a tense silence, beneath the noise on the car radio. Eventually she asked, less fiercely, 'What were you doing?'

'Painting.'
'Imagine,' she sniffed.
'No, really painting. For a change.'

'You still haven't done my room,' said Grace, who had little patience for painting for its own sake.

'I was actually getting somewhere. That's why I was late.'

'Muse popped by did she?'

'Yes. I think she did.'

Grace glanced at him despite herself. Seeing that he was serious she was quiet for a moment. Then she turned the music up, singing along to warm up her voice.

The church was small and low, lit by candles down the central aisle. Simon sat near the back of the quiet, civilised audience, while the vaulted space filled with the clean sound of voices, a harpsichord threading between them. He cast his eyes around the slate and marble plaques, the green tapestry altar cloth, the gold crucifix gleaming back at the candles. Sound cascaded down from the rafters. He closed his eyes, and colours and shapes filled his mind.

In the interval he walked out through the dark churchyard to the village, and then on down the lane towards the sound of the sea. Gorse and blackthorn scented the evening air, and glowed faintly in the starlight. Simon walked right down over the shingle to where the waves gushed over the pebbles. The tide was full, a huge mass of black water tucked between the cliffs in the darkness. Walking back he heard the echoes of singing from the church before he saw the softly-lit stained glass through the trees, a sound like the chanting of time.

The moon came out as they rolled home over the hills, and patches of milky mist appeared beside the road. Grace broke the mood:

'Why have you dumped Jo?'

'Why ... what do you mean?'

'I saw her yesterday. She looks like she's been dumped.'

'What does that look like?'

'I thought you'd know. Anyway you're stalling. You have or you haven't.'

'Isn't there a 'don't know'?'

Two aggravating adverts followed each other on the radio before Grace answered.

'Why? I thought you two were getting on really well.'

'It's been a bit difficult lately,' Simon began, aware of choosing his words carefully, ready to open up.

'Oh well, never mind,' said Grace, 'Just curious.' She began to sing along with the radio again.

Simon knew there was no point in going back to the flat, but went straight back to the studio after dropping Grace. His sketches were all over the floor, hastily made with charcoal on the backs of other unfinished work and, when he had run out of them, on the backs of invoices and bills. He put them in line on the floor in different orders, looking for a sequence that worked. In the end five stages looked right, and he fiddled and revised them with the charcoal, throwing the rejects into a corner.

He laid out five virgin white boards on tables and benches, flat. Using a couple of different sized lids from old paintpots, he delicately scribed one circle on each in a different position in a light pencil. Satisfied, he started work on a colour, mixing and mixing in an old plastic tray made for a paint roller. Time had ceased to matter. Occasionally he made another cup of coffee, went to the toilet, changed the music, but there was a lot of work to do, and he was fired up as he had not been for years. He dabbed the colour on any nearby surface, having to calculate how it would dry, too impatient to wait.

At last he turned again to the boards. There was none of the usual frisson as his brush first touched the white surface. 'Waste not, want not' the Brigadier had loved to say, carefully rationing Simon's paper supply when he was small. 'Use both sides. Never be afraid of white space,' his tutor had countermanded, 'don't let it be the boss.' Neither of them mattered this time. He knew what he wanted.

He filled every circle carefully with a deep, powerful yellow, darkened by an almost invisible swirl of almost unmixed red, lambent and full of repressed energy. The circles shone like suns from the white spaces, making them seem bare. He worked and stopped and stared, anxious not to overdo the brushwork at the expense of the action and immediacy. He stood back at last, and laughed at himself. It was late, and he was very stiff from bending over. A good night's work. Five yellow discs. How could he explain that if someone came by? No wonder artists work alone.

Back at the flat his mind was too busy for bed. He flicked late night TV channels, drank more coffee, dozed. Finally he picked himself up and staggered to bed, near dawn. He thought for a moment about Jo, but was too tired to focus. He dreamt, in reds and browns.

He had forgotten until the sun poured into the bedroom window that the next day was a working day at school. Wretchedly he crawled out of bed and hastily made himself ready to face Year Ten. He was only part-time, but the money still mattered even if the work was soul-sapping.

His first few barking outbursts told the class which way the wind was blowing. They muttered in corners, keeping away from him. Except for Stacey, who would and did say anything she liked.

'Rough night, sir?'

'Yes, as it happens. So watch out.'

'Wonder what she's looking like this morning.'

'Get on with it, Stacey.'

'Why can't we do something that isn't boring,' she whined, 'I hate interiors.' There was a chorus of disaffection.

'You paint whatever you like,' said Ian, 'all that iceberg stuff or whatever it is. It's not fair.'

'Get some work done.'

But they wouldn't. They were no more pleased to be there than he was, and happier to talk than to work.

'Why do you keep doing all those greeny things anyway?' said Sarah, 'Don't you get fed up?'

''Cos people buy them,' said Ian. 'Fuck knows why,' muttered another voice deep in the undergrowth. 'Why don't you do something different?' went on Sarah.

'Yeah, like interiors.' said someone else.

'I am trying something different, strangely enough,' said Simon in a lighter tone, which made some of the class look up.

'What is it this time? Blobs?' said Stacey, making for the door. 'I'm going to the loo by the way.'

'Why are you staring out of the window Michael?'

'Looking for inspiration, sir.'

'There it is,' said Simon, tapping his pad, 'there. That's where you'll find it. Do stuff. Even if it's rubbish. In the end you'll hit the vein.'

Michael's eyes opened wide at his metaphor. Simon had been thinking of gold mines, but Michael came from a more desperate background, and saw only blood.

'Get something down before I come round again.'

'I don't want to spoil the paper.' said Michael, 'It's perfect. Like a virgin.' Behind him one of the girls started singing 'Like a Virgin' quietly to herself.

'Just bloody do something!'

He hadn't felt his self-control start to slip. One minute he had it, the next he was brimming with petulant rage. A silence fell. No longer was he a neutral, a non-combatant in the generation game. Their closed faces stared at him; teacher, bastard.

'Get on with it.' he sighed, and turned away.

He had been working for an hour before there was a knock on the studio door. Opening the door meant going down the narrow wooden stairs. It was raining hard, the rain hitting the glass at an acute angle and rattling it with gusts. Haydn quartets were unfolding loudly from the CD player, and Simon wasn't sure how long the knocking had been going on. He didn't want to stop or talk to anyone, but eventually his curiosity to see who was standing in the rain and darkness overcame him.

When he opened the door, the lane outside was empty. Looking up the lane, he saw Jo's car turning around. The hedgerows changed from black to green through the sparkling rain as the headlights tracked over them. She started back the way she had come. At the last minute he saw her white face behind the glass, and saw that she too had seen him outlined in the door. But the car accelerated instead of stopping and rounded the corner, out of sight, fast. Then the lane was dark again, and the rain invisible.

He stood for a moment in the doorway. The subtleties of female body language mostly eluded Simon, but this one was clear enough. Follow me. Come up to the cottage. Face the music. Perhaps when I've had my say, I'll make it worth your while. He hesitated. Upstairs bowls of blood-red were waiting.

Her voice on her answerphone was bright, seeming to belong to a different person from the woebegone face in the dark. It brought him up short with surprise and something approaching shame. 'Sorry Jo. By the time I came downstairs you were leaving. I thought it was just kids knocking at the door, like they do sometimes when I'm working. I'll meet you ... tomorrow, for lunch. I'll come to the gallery. Bye.' He hung up swearing, wondering once more whether to follow her through the night.

9

The town was waking up. In the distance the sea was blue and green with an overlay of silver, bright enough to hurt the eyes. The far sand dunes were shimmering, although there was still no heat in the sun. The reality of a holiday town was everywhere. The latest signs and logos were appearing above familiar shops, as new entrepreneurs tried their luck with the high rents and short harvest-time at their disposal. Trestles and baskets of craft-ware and trash spilled into the streets, the T-shirts sporting this year's designs, the postcards, the fudge, the third world carvings, the bakeries. And now of course, every few shops, where there would once have been chancers peddling mantelpiece rubbish, there were galleries. Simon tried to avert his eyes from them as he walked by, but now and then there was something worth seeing, and more often there were paintings so bad they made him pause in his tracks to gape in wonder.

Small knots of people were already stepping aimlessly down the narrow old streets. Nice nuclear families with well dressed children were absorbing the atmosphere and culture. Local boys ran past and through them on noisy skateboards. Seagulls yawped on rooftops and swooped low down the middle of the street, yellow beaks turning this way and that, eyes keen for the annual feast to begin. From open upper windows came the smell of fresh paint and the sound of power tools as the finishing touches were put to the holiday accommodation. Simon cut along the seafront, where the harbour was brim full, calm and enticing. On such a morning it was possible once again to remember why people would travel and suffer and pay through the nose to be here.

Ti, who owned Jo's gallery, was a tall and elegant woman in her early sixties. She wore expensive clothes in natural colours, silver hair and jewellry, beautiful shoes, and had a sculpted face which made her seem other-worldly. She always held a little pause before answering a question, so that conversation with her was a little like an international telephone call. It invited others to interrupt, and then feel clumsy for doing so. Her pronouncements seemed more considered than other people's, and together with her height, made her gently intimidating. Her still beautiful smile had a permanent note of forgiveness for the crudeness of human kind.

Richard, her husband, was her link to mother earth and saving grace, though graceless in himself. He looked like what he was, a successful heating contractor, shorter than Ti, comfortably stout, and loud. He knew nothing of art and had no pretensions. He loved Ti with the passion of a man who still couldn't believe his luck, and financed her aspirations generously. In return she allowed herself to unwind with him occasionally in a dignified way. The gallery was in a converted fish cellar in a back lane, and lost a little money each year, but it provided an outlet for Ti's delicate silver jewellry and other refined but barely commercial works.

Simon breezed in, greeting Jo as if everything was normal. Before he could whisk her off, Ti stopped him.

'Simon dear, I hear you're deep into your new work ...'

'Yes, flat out, Ti. My exhibition's quite soon.'

'Mm. I was wondering ... if you would like to try them out ... have a little pre-release as it were. We could find you some wallspace here, while they ... got on their feet ...?'

'Nice thought. I'd have to see what Andrew has to say. It could get a little bow wave going before I open in London.' He frowned slightly. 'Of course I wouldn't be able to sell …' A pause fell.

'I know darling. I know. When will you have something to show?'

'Couple of weeks at the rate I'm working.' Jo looked up sharply.

'Change of style?' said Ti.

'Oh yes. You'll see.'

Ti was careful not to express too much pleasure at this, in case it reflected a judgement on his previous work. Simon was turning to go with Jo, who still had not spoken a word, when Richard bumbled in.

'Hello Simon. You've been a bit of a stranger round here. How's the leg and the rest of it?'

Simon assured him he was now fine.

'Good,' said Richard, 'Poor Jo's been pining away!'

The three others looked quickly at Richard to see how much should be read into his remark. There was a moment's utter silence, until the phone rang. Ti took it, and waved Simon and Jo away with the other hand as she settled into a long and mostly passive conversation. Richard smiled broadly and uncomprehendingly as they fled.

Faced with a choice of cafes, pizzerias, pasty and fish and chip shops and pricey restaurants, they chose the back of one of the secondary pubs. A baffling gambling machine lit the gloom. The music was loud, which made private conversation possible. They ordered drinks and food with awkward formality. Jo was determined not to raise the subject of painters or painting. So she just said, 'You're better.'

'Just about. Still sore in the joints, but the bits that show are nearly as good as new. At least I can work again …'

'Nadia's been staying with me.'

This unwelcome news diverted Simon for a moment. Nadia and Simon had disliked each other at first sight. No doubt they had been spending happy hours together dragging his name through the mud. Simon nodded wisely. '... but she's gone back now.'

'I've been so busy ...' said Simon, leaving an opening a tank could drive through.

'It's been good to have someone I can really talk to,' Jo went on.

'I'm sorry to have been so useless,' said Simon. 'It's been a bad time. But something good's come out of it.'

'My mum was going to come down too. But I put her off. She doesn't miss much. And she's been warning me not to get pregnant since I was thirteen.'

Simon was finally derailed.

'Does she know?'

'What's to know?' said Jo, smiling and furious.

'Well – that you're – you are still aren't you?'

'Nice you should ask. It's quite important to me actually. Almost as important as wiping smears of paint onto bits of canvas.' Just then hostilities had to be suspended as the teenage waitress brought their food.

'Thank you.'

'Thank you.'

For a few moments they ate in silence. Then Jo looked up.

'You've got over it, haven't you, whatever it was. You're better. It's me that can't sleep.'

'I have not got over it. You have no idea ...'

'Well perhaps I don't care any more. My problems are more – are less – abstract. If you want it in simple bullet points, we had a relationship – quite good I thought – we conceived a child – you freaked out and went and fell down a hole – we've hardly spoken since. OK so far?'

Simon nodded dumbly.

'So all I can think about,' – she stopped to sip her drink – 'is, do I owe it to this – forthcoming human – to have it, maybe as a single mum, maybe ruining my own life, maybe hating it every time it reminds me of its father? Or do I check 'No thanks' and put a stop to its little life right now?'

Simon was silent.

'And I thought it might be nice to know what you think, since you've invested all that DNA in it and all, quite willingly as I remember.' She took a mouthful of food. It was good, even for a few moments, to see Simon caught in the headlights. Simon took a drink, and paused.

'I don't know what to say, Jo.' She kept on eating, occasionally looking at him with an expression of friendly enquiry. He felt the walls closing in. 'I don't think it's even right for me to say. If I said get rid of it, you'd think that's just the easy way out. If I said keep it you'd tell me … it's you not me that has to give birth to it, and look after it, and be its mother. You see?' He felt the ground firming under his feet. It was true. What could he possibly say?

Jo stopped eating and looked disconcertingly straight into his face. 'Strange as it may seem, Simon, I wasn't looking for the right answer, or even the clever answer. I know that what you said is right. If all I needed was common sense, I could have stayed at home and talked to myself.'

'So what do you want me to say?'

'What you feel!' she said, and banged her drink down on the table so hard that their cutlery rattled.

'I can manage the logic,' she went on, 'I've had plenty of time to think. But I don't know what's happening in there' – she pointed at his head – 'or in there' – she pointed at his heart.

Simon was about to reply, but she went straight on. 'That's what I need to know. Deep in your gut do you actually secretly fancy having a child of your own? Especially after bringing up someone else's? Or are you truly madly deeply wetting yourself and waiting for me to say OK, it's all over, all clear, everyone get on with your lives? As you were? How am I supposed to tell from your … mask?'

Simon bit his lip. He shut his eyes, and at once the silent face in the orange mud swam before his eyes.

'I'm sorry Jo, but I've got to go with what you think. I can't make you feel you have to have a baby because of me. Or that you have to get rid of it because of me.'

'I'm pregnant because of you.'

'I know.'

Jo went back to the gallery on her own. In the back street she saw the Howard making his leisurely way down towards her. It was too late to go back. Howard parked himself in a comfortable, anticipatory way, his linen jacket open over his black T-shirt, his hair still unfashionably long.

'Ah Jo, hello,' he started, 'have the first explorers penetrated Ti's private sanctum yet?'

'Sorry, I'm a bit late Howard.'

'And how is the boy wonder? Has he tried any more experiments in unassisted flight?'

'Can't stop.' She swept past him with an attempted smile. Howard remained in the same position for a moment after she had gone.

But he was at a loose end. Half an hour later he entered the quiet gallery, gave Jo a polite nod and padded soundlessly around the exhibits. After a while she could no longer sustain the pretence of being busy.

'Have you known Simon long?'

'Ever since he blew into Jane's life, pretty little thing that he was,' said Howard without turning round. 'I didn't see it lasting.'

'Why?'

Howard paused and gazed again at a shiny pottery vase, feeling its texture with a fingertip.

'I didn't really see him as someone with any … substance. Whereas Jane is all substance. I suppose that's why it worked, if I think about it.'

The slippery fish again. Did everyone see him like that?

'Did Jane have a lot of relationships before?' she asked, feeling nosy and prim.

'Well there was Neil of course. Apart from that? Yes, pretty much when she felt like it. Like an Indian take-away. Depending of course on what you mean by a relationship,' he added with an arch grin. 'With me that's anything over forty minutes, but I know others take these things more seriously. She wasn't promiscuous in that sense. Choosy.'

A silence fell. Howard wandered towards the door. He gave Jo a kindly look. 'Not an easy boy. Needs a firm hand. Preferably grasping a short whip. I've offered of course …'
Jo did not smile.

'And perhaps not the ideal basket to tip all your eggs into, dear thing. Carpe diem and all that.'
He held out his soft hand and Jo shook it, seeing a good intention.

'Thank you,' she said.
Howard gave a small bow before exiting. She stared at the door for a long time after he had gone, thinking about eggs and baskets.

10

The bright blood-red was shining. All the paintings were dry. Simon left them alone, and went to find some more bits of old canvas and board, things he had spoiled or hated too much to finish. One of the first lessons he had learned was that if you mix all the colours together you end up with a deep brown sludge. That was what he wanted now, so he threw in everything until the mixture was like dull wet earth. He bled in a little more red and ochre until the tone seemed right. He wanted a colour which was the enemy of natural light, greedily matt and absorbent. Taking more bowls, he watered the colour down into looser and looser consistencies, keeping all of them.

He divided one of his old white boards into sections, and tried different mixtures on each. Some sections he brushed first with linseed oil, some he scraped with candlewax. It wasn't coming. He put a little washing-up liquid into one mixture, olive oil into another, even some off milk into another, simple adhesive into another. He laid out one board flat and poured a mixture onto it, pushing it this way and that as it dried.

It was late but he worked on. The sections slowly began to dry. Too slowly. There was a hairdryer which Simon had brought here once in an emergency when very late for an opening. He turned it on and played it over the experiments. Near, but still not right.

He thought of ever odder concoctions, like porridge, sawdust, the contents of the vacuum cleaner. He dismissed them all. Just as he was flagging, he remembered some clay he was storing for a potter. He dug a little out of its polythene sack. It was deep earthenware red, just what he had been looking for. He beat it in water and glue until it was sloppy and then tried it in different combinations with the rest. He sang to keep himself awake as the hairdryer whirred again. He held it close to the ruddy pools and turned up the power so that the air pushed them about, leaving a swirly, crusty residue. Each was different. He waited. He walked outside in the dark to cool his tired sweat. He turned the radio off, infuriated by its twitter, and worked in silence. At last he laid down to rest in a sleeping bag on the old broken sofa.

Two hours later he got up. Natural light was beginning to brighten the skylights. He felt like a teenager after a rough party, but as soon as he had cleared his eyes with cold water, he stared hard at every one of his tests. He ran a finger gently over the textures. Two or three batches had turned out well. The ochre had pooled and parted, defined itself in small globules and larger lines of matter, mats of pure colour and small archipelagos in an almost translucent sea.

He checked the notes of the mixture, sparing a grateful thought that it wasn't the one with the milk. He beat up the best replica he could devise with a glue, and then without pausing brushed it thickly over the yellow and red and white of his first painting. As it congealed he held it up at all angles and gently shook it, so that the colour ran in every direction. He covered the rest and did the same.

He could not bear to watch them dry, so he walked back to his flat through the deserted early-morning streets. The first rays of the sun were just touching the gold lichen on the roofs. He showered, and crawled naked into bed, oblivious to the seagulls' morning chorus.

Jane was looking forward to seeing Simon at Maria's private view. Private views had been the parentheses of their relationship. They had met at one and broken up at another. Now all that was left was the occasional desire to send him up. It wasn't usually difficult. He was vulnerable anywhere along the fragile borders of his ego if you knew where to strike, which she did.

Their parting had been coming for a long time, but she had been determined to pre-empt the last rites. She had wanted it to be quite obvious to the small society who may have cared just who was leaving who. The screaming match at the otherwise quiet little gallery on the seafront had been stage-managed in advance. She had decided which buttons to press. Her speeches had been rehearsed, while he just spluttered. As her voice rose and the background conversation ceased, he had become shrill and uncontrolled. Poor Natasha, whose new collection of daguerreotypes had formed the unwilling background to their terminal drama, had put her hands dramatically over her ears as the intimate stuff had flown across the crowded and fascinated room. The lutenist halted in mid-madrigal. Eventually Simon had thrown his glass furiously to the floor. Unfortunately it landed on an Iranian rug and didn't smash but merely bounced once or twice, adding farce to the occasion. He fled from her life.

She scrabbled through her disorganised box of earrings, looking for a pair she was not tired of. Upstairs Grace and Stacey were shouting at each other over thunderously loud music, and she yelled ineffectually at them to turn it down. The hour was sufficiently late. Howard was waiting downstairs, as he had been for a while.

The gallery was very full, and thick with the smell of incense and cannabis. Maria, the star of the evening, had never betrayed her inner child. She was in her customary kaftan, her hair still long and girlishly wild, although she was well over sixty. The other elements were standard private view fare – the red 'n white choice, the nibbles, the crudites – the jazz guitarist – the same cast of faces – and the huge and awful swirly red abstracts for which Maria had somehow managed to find a market.

'Covers a big damp patch,' Howard whispered in Jane's ear, at which she gave a wolfish grin.

'Jane!' said a loud voice, as if surprised to see her.

'Hello Maria.'

Maria's kaftan was silver, with a deep cleavage over her thin brown chest. 'Darling,' she cooed, 'so glad you could make it. And Howard too. Wow. What are you working on at the moment darling?'

The question was addressed at Howard, and intentionally cruel. For a short time, long ago, Howard had been half of a successful TV writing team, which had made him wealthy and famous. His partner had then left him for a songwriter in San Francisco, and with him went the magic touch. Nothing Howard had tried since had worked, neither new comedy situations nor new partners. He had diversified, written a novel and some plays, but by then the drink was soaking up what talent he had left. They all failed. His only success was a sideline in art criticism, which together with his repeat fees kept the wolf half a pace from the door.

Jane had come to him as an actress in one of his short-lived shows, desperate for accommodation in London, but already perfectly self-possessed. She had moved in for a week and stayed for years. Their friendship was true and deep, and had weathered many other partners on each side. He had followed her down to Cornwall, and had been a frequent umpire in her long match with Simon. He had also been an attempted good uncle to Grace; and was genuinely grieved when it had all finally fallen apart.

'Just perfecting the haiku at the moment. Want to hear one?'

'Love to,' she cooed, turning away. 'What do you think of the show darling?' she went on to Jane. She knew Jane's view of her work, but it was her evening, and she knew that even Jane could not criticise her while drinking her wine.

'I don't know how you do it.'

Their teeth flashed at each other.

'Hope you're going to be nice Howard. I always read your stuff with such a thrill of apprehension. Are you picking up my latest vibe?'

God, thought Howard, it's bad enough that people really spoke to each other like that when she was young, let alone now.

'I'm expecting to pick something up very soon.'

'Groovy. Hello sweetheart.'

She had gone.

Private views had lost their appeal for Jane after the first three or four, but she still went. Everyone still went. The venues changed, the stuff on the wall was different, but the faces remained familiar. If anyone new turned up the whole assembly registered them with an almost predatory interest.

Simon had once been that fresh scent. Jane had noticed him around the town, as anyone was sure to be noticed out of season. He had blonde hair and a blonde girlfriend, and she had taken him for just another surf zombie. But late one evening he had wandered in off the street into one of Lawrence's – now Sir Lawrence's – endless series of retrospectives. Charcoal on paper, she remembered. The girlfriend was not at his side.

They stood together in front of a sketch of a hawthorn tree. The crowd had thinned a little and it was actually possible to see the work.

'He's got a good free wrist, hasn't he?'

As a line it was absurdly lame but it was an opening. She turned around and faced him. She was tall, full-breasted, with a challenging stare. Most men quailed a little or made a foolish remark while under the force of her gaze, but Simon just stood and, after a few moments gave an open grin.

'Sorry. Is he a relation of yours or something? I'm still getting used to the fact that everyone around here knows everyone else.'

'Do you know a lot about art?' Jane's voice was unexpectedly deep and warm, though the words were as challenging as the look.

'I paint.'

Jane gave a look of disappointment, saying clearly enough: not another one. Her eyes were deep brown, almost black.

'Come to get some Cornish credibility under your belt?'

'I hadn't thought of it like that. I only came for a visit. I didn't mean to stay.'

'Beware. You'll wake up one day and find you're middle-aged and the grass has grown right up to your waist. It happens to people here.'

'Oh, no,' said the young man, 'I'm definitely moving on in a few days. I have to get out of my flat anyway, before the first visitors come.'

'I've got a spare room.'

He looked up sharply, not sure that he had heard. She was sipping her glass, looking up once again at the hawthorn bush. She turned to him in enquiry, not a hint of seduction in her face.

'That's very kind of you. Where do you live?'

Jane lived in a big terraced house not far from the centre of town, with a view of the harbour from the attic room and a sunny garden with an apple tree. Neil, her ex, had left her with Grace in one hand and the house-keys in the other, and she had called it quits. Neil was dead now. The Land Rover had filled the country lane as he rounded the corner, and the motor-bike had had nowhere to go but straight into it. Jane had the house, and Grace, the life insurance he hadn't got around to cancelling, and the rent from a former aunt's house in Sussex. She did also occasionally take in paying guests. She got by.

She gave Simon the address and they talked for a little longer. Then she went home alone and sat reading over a cup of coffee until the door bell rang.

At first Simon was disconcerted to be shown the spare room. They shared some coffee, talked more, then Jane sent him upstairs. When he heard her settle into her own bed he knocked softly on her door.

'Simon,' Jane's voice came clearly through the door, with no inflection of approval or rejection.

'Yes ...'

'I say when. And if.'

'Oh ... right.'

'Goodnight.'

Grace had scarcely looked at Simon over breakfast, and easily brushed off his attempts to make her smile. Even at six she could look though men as if they were patches of mist. Simon went out each day and sketched. Jane did not accompany him, but they ate together in the evening and warmed to each other with ease. She was surprised at his work, and quite impressed. It had more life and enthusiasm than she was used to in a hothouse artistic community, almost gauche in its freshness. She was only a few years older, but felt the tenderness of a generation between them.

Simon slept lightly, but was taken by surprise one night to awaken and find her sitting on his bed, looking thoughtfully down at him. A faint light from the hall lay on his face, though hers was in shadow, and he could not see her expression. He reached up strongly for her, but she put his arms firmly back onto the bed.

'Sshhh ...' she said.

She gently traced the outline of his face with her fingers. She bent over and kissed his lips gently, her hair flowing around their faces. He reached up more slowly and took her head in his hands, carefully, as if afraid to break it. When the kiss was over, she folded aside his duvet. With one delicate finger she pulled lightly at the bottom of the T-shirt which was all he wore. Obediently he drew it over his head. He was growing accustomed to the light, and could see that her eyes were still slightly frowning, as if trying to solve a spiritual puzzle, not shining but deepening. He felt himself sinking into them.

She was naked beneath a linen dressing gown. He put his arms around her warm waist beneath it. The dressing gown slipped to the floor. They kissed again, long and deeply and slowly.

'Is this when?' he said.

'This is when.'

The evening was becoming tiresome. Howard was paying exaggerated court to a young Dutch potter. Everyone else seemed to be talking about money. Angela had spent twenty minutes describing her latest alternative therapy at the top of her voice, Adrian and Sven had described their new bathroom, Ti had paused as if to speak but only gave an extra-terrestrial smile, Ralph was roaring drunk and handling any woman who wasn't fast enough, Vaughan was standing alone in the corner, hooded eyes cast down into his drink and vast black beard obscuring the rest of his features, as usual.

Everything was as usual. Simon hadn't come, so there was not even that sour grape to suck on. What was the American term ... SNAFU? ... Situation Normal, All Fucked Up. Here it was ... SNJFS ... Situation Normal, Just the Fucking Same. Not very easy to remember, SNJFS ... not easy to say either ... perhaps she could do better if she tried ... it finally dawned on Jane how drunk she was. She made for the door. She made little waving movements with her fingers across the room at Maria and soundlessly mouthed 'The pictures are shite, darling'. Maria waved a little finger back.

Jane thumped Howard as she passed, making him spill his drink over the potter. He looked up and gave Jane a quick, grateful smile before fussing over the potter with his handkerchief. She clopped through the empty streets on her own, occasional white-bellied gulls still flying overhead and the murmuring sound of the sea in the air.

11

There is a quiet and selfish time for artists when a piece has been finished, but no-one else has seen it.

Like all the rest, Simon had learned the hard way that the most important decision was when to stop. New ideas were always crowding around, plus dissatisfaction with what was there, doubt as to whether to try another way or a bit more of this or that. It was partly confidence which allowed Simon to clean his brushes, and partly experience. There was a time to let go and walk away, and choosing that moment was always significant. On a bad day it was merely an abandonment to fate. On a good one the act of stopping was almost dramatic, a flourish of its own.

Then for the first and last time the work would be perfect, like the morning after a snowfall. No-one else had dragged their feet across it, leaving traces of their opinion. It had not been through the mill of liking and disliking, or quite liking, or not really my thing. Mothers must feel this sensation times a thousand, Simon thought. So that's what was inside me. Hello.

The five paintings stared challengingly back at him. They would not stay new. He might never show them to anyone, but hide or destroy them, desperate – like all artists – that no-one should know how bad he could be if he tried. If he was satisfied he would put his name to them, and they would take their place in his catalogue, never again as important as they were now. Artist and work glared at each other.

Four of them worked. The fifth should have been the climax, but wasn't. It was alright, but the sequence left an emptiness, something lacking. Simon made more coffee and looked at a magazine for a while, just to shift the images behind his eyes. Then he looked up again directly at *No 5*, and saw what it lacked.

It was courage. He saw again the simple shape in the darkness, calling to him over the dark, still pool. Take courage. Take a risk. Do what you must. Help me.

He mixed up a small pool of ivory paint. Moving to the right of the frame, he took a full brush. The first line was always the worst, defining all the others. Using his whole arm, Simon painted a clean curve of ivory over the muddy brown. He stopped, to be sure the balance and dynamic were working. The line was good. He began to fill the colour in.

Andrew Statham rang next morning.
    'Simon,'
    'Hello, Andrew.'
    'Hate to say this, but have you actually done anything? Anything I can look at? I'm getting just a tad anxious. I'm coming down this weekend anyway. I mean, do say if you've done bugger-all, but time's getting a little short ...'
    'I've just finished the first batch of my new stuff. They're drying now.'
    'How many?'
    'Five.'

Andrew gave a deep sigh and said nothing for a moment. Then he spoke with an even more world-weary voice.
    'New ... ?'

'Yes, I've only done five at the moment, but they really are going somewhere. I'll try and do some more this week.'

'New as in … a new style?'

'You won't believe it.'

'Simon, what about some new … old stuff?'

'Well I haven't done any of that. I suppose I'm changing direction.'

Andrew paused for a long time.

'One could fault your timing. It's your current direction which has opened doors for you.'

'Yes, I know that.'

'I suppose we can recycle to a limited extent. But it won't fool the sharper eyes. Well, do a batch of the traditional stuff as well, will you? Just to be … on the safe side. You know, they're your … signature, they …'

'Sell?'

'To put it crudely, they do sell. And I am taking a financial risk here, and so is the gallery.'

'But what about my art?' said Simon in an outraged tone.

' Um … er … the thing is …'

'Oh come on, Andrew, I'm taking the piss. I'll hack you out a few icebergs before you come down. But you must promise to put the new stuff up too.'

Andrew's sigh had a note of relief in it.

'Mmm,' he said non-committally, 'I'll certainly look at them with an open mind.'

Simon was as good as his word and turned the drying paintings away, reaching for his familiar range of colours. He worked hard all afternoon laying out new pieces, and into the evening. Then he suddenly realised he was hungry. He grabbed his coat and hurried out of the studio.

There was plenty of space in the pasta house on the harbour-side, and he sat on his own by the window. The lights around the harbour quivered in the water of a full tide, and there were some people on the streets, heralding the beginning of a seasonal buzz. Simon ordered an expensive bottle of wine and sat sipping it like a solitary king, watching the boats wandering at their moorings in the gathering dark.

As the reflections in the window hardened, he spotted Howard taking dinner with a ratty-looking man in a discreet corner booth behind him. Expansively he picked up his bottle and went to join them, conscious at once of Howard's irritation and the ratty one's confusion as to his motives.

'Ah, Simon dear heart, this is Kevin. So pleased to see you all better.'

'Hello,' said Kevin. His voice was unchipped Glasgow with a furtive edge.

'Have you known each other long?' said Simon pleasantly.
The Scot looked at Howard, uncertain how to reply. But Howard had no such scruples.

'Oh, it must be all of a couple of hours, mustn't it Kevin. I was feeling rejected after an abortive liaison with a charming Dutch fellow, but then I bumped into Kevin ...' I can guess where, thought Simon ' ... and decided it was time I cheered myself up.'

'Ah.'

'Simon's an artist, Kevin. Who isn't, of course, but he does have a certain repute. He can sell paintings without putting dragons or mermaids or – what are those bloody fish called – dolphins on them. Bit cold though. But clever.'

'Do you paint, Kevin?' said Simon to fill a yawning gap, but it only made matters worse.

'No,' said Kevin, shutting his mouth again hard, like a trap.

'Kevin earns an honest living, Simon. He plasters houses; and before you sneer, his work stays on the walls a sight longer than most stuff, even yours.'

Howard seemed blurred with drink. He looked old and tired, red around the eyes, and blue beneath. Simon knew him well in this state and made to escape. But Howard needed him to stay.

'Sit down for Christ's sake,' he said, pulling at Simon's arm. 'I'm afraid Kevin's bored with me,' he added in a stage whisper.

Kevin ate quickly, with a survivor's instinct. If the party was about to break up he would at least make sure he had a decent meal inside him.

'Do I gather you've gone off the lovely Josephine?' Howard went on rudely, biting hard on a spiced meatball.

'What's the occasion, your birthday or something?' said Simon to change the subject.

'My birthday is a national holiday, dear boy, as you know, marked in all good diaries. You should cultivate this lad, Kevin. Face of an angel. Heart of a whore. Cock like an iron bar. Bum like peach fuzz on ...'

'Shut up Howard.'

' ... Sadly immune to my blandishments. So far. Susceptible to money though. And flattery.'

Simon rose again, but Howard pulled him down even harder. 'Don't mind me,' he said. 'Let's go somewhere and talk. I'll get rid of McTavish here, and we can have a nice chat.' Kevin's face was impassive as he finished his glass of wine.

'Who said I've finished with Jo?'

'Mystic Meg.'

'Bloody Jane I suppose.

Howard cleaned his plate with a bread roll, then dabbed his face with a napkin. 'Kevin,' he said reasonably, 'would you be an absolute angel and fuck off?' Kevin's eyes did the rounds between the two of them, then decided to cut his losses. He suddenly stood up to go.

As he hurried away Simon looked more closely at Howard. He was very drunk and in the mood for viciousness, but there was another, unfamiliar tone in his voice. He looked at Simon for a moment, focussing slowly, then leant over and put his hand firmly on Simon's thigh. Simon didn't flinch.

'Get your head out of your arse dear boy.'

'Look who's talking.'

Howard began to laugh, softly and without edge. 'Touché', he said and laughed again, his face suddenly boyish. But the laughter went on too long, and Simon watched the years pile back on as it changed to tears.

'Oh God,' said Howard into his plate, 'the old drunk's crying. Take to the boats.' His hand stayed on Simon's thigh. Simon patted it.

'You're alright, Howard. Calm down.'

Howard blew his nose and kept the handkerchief over his face until his breathing returned to normal.

'I'm sorry dear boy.'

'What's the matter?'

'Give the girl another chance. Think of someone else for a change. You're such a selfish little prick.'

There was no offence in the words. Simon tried again to head him off. 'What's the matter? Tell me.'

Howard ran a hand through his crinkly grey hair.

'Lump. In the bollocks. Went to the doctor this morning. Want to feel it?'

'No thanks.'

'Seeing the specialist next week.'

'You'll be alright.'

Simon smiled reassuringly. Howard's voice suddenly gained strength.

'Fuck you, Simon. I've a terrible urge to slap your face until it bleeds.' His hand was a claw in Simon's thigh. 'You've always had it too soft. You don't know what life's about. You'll see one day. Then you won't think it's such a bloody hay-ride.'

'It might be nothing.'

'So it might.' He was looking straight at Simon and his voice had risen. 'And it might also be my notice to quit. My cards – no, you won't remember cards. My lifetime's achievement, piss-off-and-die award. The nice rich specialist will look at me and say 'Bye bye, old chap, thanks for cheering people up a bit. Try not to linger and incur the NHS a lot of unnecessary expense' What a piss-up there'll be.'

Tears were squeezing from the sides of his eyes again. Please God, thought Simon, let me fall under a bus or be killed by a jealous lover, bitten by a poisonous snake, stabbed by a crazed mugger, or anything. Please don't let me end up as a drunken bore weeping away my days in a seaside restaurant.

'I'm going now,' said Simon.
'My voice may be a little higher next time you see me,' Howard was attempting to bounce back. 'My days as a famous seducer may be over, but there'll be a place for me in the male voice choir. In the counter-tenors of course. Take care, dear boy. You mean a lot to me.' The blood rushed back into Simon's leg as Howard finally released his grip. He fled. He stopped by the studio, not able to leave things alone.

Grace was on the answerphone. 'Simon, I need to see you straight away.' It was late, but she answered at once.

The script was familiar. She had had a furious row with Jane, about nothing at all. She was grounded, like a ten-year-old. Jane wouldn't give her any money. She was fed up with being treated like a stupid kid. She couldn't wait to leave home, she was counting the days. Could she come and stay at the flat?
No was the obvious answer, but Simon wanted to think of a softer presentation. There was a pause.
'Where are you?' she said
'At the studio.'

'I'll come up.'

'No, wait ...' He was talking to himself.

There was also an answerphone message from Jo:

'Just thought you'd like an update on how the family's getting on. I've got my first appointment with the doctor next week. I've got to have two counselling sessions before I'm allowed an abortion, to ensure I'm not acting on the spur of the moment. As if. They'll want to know what you think about it all, and you're entitled to counselling too if you can get your head out of your arse for long enough. Ça va. Bye.'

She was the second person in an hour to rebuke him with the same gross image.

Grace knocked on the door, and he went down to let her in. Since he had last seen her she had cut her hair shorter and knotted it in small black-dyed knots. Despite the night's chill, she was wearing a short slight top, and her navel ring shone in the streetlight. Her face wore its usual pallor, and she looked even thinner than usual, a feral creature of the night.

'I'm making cocoa. Do you want some?' She nodded as she sat down on the arm of the broken sofa.

'Can you let me have some money? I really need it.'

She waited for the question why. But it didn't come. Simon looked at her closely, then handed over two twenty-pound notes. She looked at the money twice to be sure, before tucking it into her jeans. Then she looked back at Simon, the aggression still in her face.

'Thanks.' There was a pause. 'What, no lecture?'

'No.'

'OK. Wow. I'm not used to this. Something wrong?'

'No.'

'Oh. Right.' Having won without a fight, she felt he could not leave straight away. She pondered further.

'Is it just to spite Jane?'

'I don't want her to know I gave it to you. Please tell me it isn't for drugs.'

'It really isn't for drugs.'

'Here's your cocoa.'

'Thanks.' The first sip made her suddenly realise how cold she was, and she gave a shiver. The cocoa was sweet and delicious. She had not eaten all day. Simon was still looking at her with an expression she could not make out. Clumsily she looked for a reciprocal gesture.

'How's your stuff getting on?'

'Fine. I've just finished some new ones.'

'What, the usual sort?'

'No. Different.'

'Can I see?'

Simon bit back the sarcasm in his mouth. Grace had spent her life in the company of art and artists, and consequently despised both with a passion. She was just trying to be nice. But someone had to be the first to see them, and she was one of the few people he cared about.

'Are you sure?'

'Yeah.'

'OK. Turn away for a minute while I set them up.'

Grace turned away while Simon pulled and scraped around with easels and pieces of furniture, propping up the paintings in a semi-circle so that she could see them more or less one at a time.

'Come on,' she said, 'Hurry up'.

'Don't look yet.' said Simon as he finished setting up. 'They're in a sequence from left to right.'

He took her hand, and she kept her other hand over her eyes, pantomime-style, as he led her in front of the first painting.

'Open.'

12

Jo looked out into the moonlit garden. Slip was hassling for a late walk so she pulled on her coat and went outside. Darkness had never bothered her, especially at the cottage. She went out of the garden and set off across the moor, walking briskly against the cold. The terrier darted in and out of the shadows cast by the gorse. After a while she realised she was close to the old mine-shaft, Simon's nemesis. It still had not been properly covered, due to a legal dispute over who exactly was responsible. A few fresh strands of shiny barbed wire and a warning notice from the council were its only marker. They were almost at the spot where she had first heard Simon's distorted and terrified voice coming out of the earth that morning. Curiosity took her towards it.

The dog suddenly stopped. He began to growl softly. He walked a few stiff steps towards the shaft and growled again, deeper and louder. Jo peered into the shadowy clearing which the rescuers had created in the undergrowth.

Someone was standing there, by the barbed wire. It was a bulky figure, wearing a coat and hood, very still and apparently staring at the ground. Jo froze. The figure was in silhouette, and she could not tell if it was male or female. Her heart began to beat in her ears as she stood still also, not breathing. Then Slip ran towards the figure, barking furiously. Jo saw a sudden white face, and then the figure ran heavily off down the path in the opposite direction, feet pounding on the stone. The dog followed a short way then ran back to Jo, pleased at his work.

Jo's whole body was trembling. She turned and half-walked, half-ran back to the cottage. She ran inside and locked the door, then checked the other doors. She closed the windows, and turned the window-locks. She had never been afraid there before. Her breathing recovered. She made some coffee, but drank a glass of brandy. She turned on the radio for courage, and sat for a long time in front of the fire. When she went up to bed, she took the dog with her. At last she fell asleep, fingers still curled in fear.

'Wow. What's happened to the North Pole and all that? It's very weird. It's not the Eclipse is it? It's so big.'

The first painting was reddish-brown, fading to dark purple at the edges. A bright yellow circle was indicated but not all visible, barely shining through curtains of streaky brown. Patterns showed within the circle, but without determinate shape or colour, except that a flash of red showed through a tiny clear point, like a sudden high note in a slow movement.

The second and third were variations on the first. In the third the circle had become distorted into more of a disc, as if it had started to rotate on its axis. The colours became progressively clearer through the overlapping murk, the yellow circle and the fractured red shapes, some clearly another way up from a previous view. In the fourth painting the red markings had become recognisable as a crude smiley face, set at an angle to the vertical. The reds and yellows were still slightly obscured, but hurtingly bright where visible. On the side of the fourth painting another hidden shape in a ghostly ivory was starting to intrude.

Grace had stopped twittering. She was turning her head, but

otherwise stock still. 'One more,' said Simon.

The fifth painting showed the smiling face almost clear, still besmirched but with most of the yellow brightening fiercely almost to white against the brown and purple background, and the red as scarlet as fresh blood. But that was not the principal figure. On the right the ivory shape had intruded even further, brighter, a slow curve, bulbous, widening as it rose and then curling away to the edge, featureless except for a dark oval shadow high up, leading out of the picture. The eye followed it irresistibly, searching vainly for the unseen remainder.

Grace had said nothing aloud, but in front of the fourth picture she swore softly to herself. She remained in front of the fifth for a long time, very quiet and still, suddenly small. When she finally turned around, Simon was amazed to see her eyes were glassy in her pale face. Grace didn't cry.

'I don't really like them, Simon,' she said at last in a choked voice. 'Sorry and all that. Especially that one.' She inclined her head towards the last painting. 'I mean, I think they're fucking brilliant and I can't believe you did them, but ... well, I wouldn't really want them on my wall,' she finished, smiling through her emotion.

'Thanks anyway,' said Simon. 'I'm glad you saw them first.'

'Yeah,' she said awkwardly. 'Well. Better go I suppose. Thanks for the money.'

She smiled again, and then went down the stairs and out, slipping back into the night.

'Are you still off coffee Jo?' Nadia sang out from the kitchen.

' 'Fraid so.'

'What else have we got. Rosehip? Ugh, ginseng. Orange? Orange!'

'Peppermint, thanks.'

Jo sat at the wooden table in her white bathrobe, her hair still wet from the shower. Nadia brought in the drinks, her slight figure already dressed in T-shirt and jeans. The windows and the door were open and Spring scents were drifting in from the garden.

'Thanks for coming down.'

'You keep saying that,' said Nadia. 'It's no hardship' She looked around the small granite room with its open fireplace and wooden floors, and out into the sunny garden. 'Did you sleep OK?'

'First time this week. It makes all the difference having someone here.' They exchanged secure smiles, but Jo was still angry inside. She hadn't needed anyone there before. She and Slip could lie on the rug and watch late night horror movies together and still go out into the garden in the dark.

Later they walked up to the mine shaft. An invisible lark was singing its bright, circular song and the air was warm.

'Doesn't look very spooky now does it?' said Jo, feeling silly.

'Everything's different at night. Where was it standing?'

'Let's see. I was up there, and so it would have beeeennnn ... here.'

'Right,' said Nadia with authority 'Stand back. I intend to examine the scene. With forensic skill. CSI and all that.' She made a pantomime of passing over the ground with a magnifying glass. 'Nothing to show. But wait. Aha. Elementary. Your intruder was a short bald man with a Swedish accent and a rusty penknife.'

'Not worth asking home for a shag then.'

'The killer's name is Arg.'

'What?'

'That's what they used to say in stories when I was a kid.'

'Arg?'

'That's how they wrote it. With lots of Hs at the end. You know, getting topped before they could ... Hello, what's this?' Her voice had gone out of character.

'What?'

'Someone's sorry they came.'

Nadia was looking at the barbed wire close to the ground. A small piece of red material was clinging to one of the points of the wire. Jo came to see.

'It's not torn,' she said neutrally. Then she walked slowly away and sat down on a rock, staring at nothing.

'You OK Jo?' said Nadia with concern. Jo nodded. Nadia bent over to look more closely at the scrap of material. She could see that, as Jo said, the cloth had been scissor cut rather than torn, into a small oblong. It was hooked neatly over the shining wire, with no sign of damage. It was a soft red cloth, with what looked like a fragment of a cartoon character printed on it. She couldn't think of anything to say. Above them the lark piped on without a break.

'Nady, what's going on?'

'I dunno. There's too many weird people around here. I feel safer in Camden Town.'

She came across and looked carefully at Jo, frowning beneath her short dark hair. 'It's alright, Jo. It's just some kind of token. A woman's. Nothing serious. Why am I telling you this? They're your rural nutters not mine. We just have the usual muggers and drive-bys and serial killers.'

'I'm not coming up here again.'

'OK. Let's go back. There are plenty of other places to walk.'

Jo was already on her way up the path. Nadia caught her up. 'Can you still drink in your condition?' she said.

'Course I can,' said Jo. 'I shouldn't but I can.'

'Let's go out tonight,' said Nadia, 'do the town, check the talent and all that. Let's leave all this weird countryside stuff to those who need it. Especially bloody great holes in the ground.'

Like Grace, Andrew Statham tarried for a long time in front of *Painting No 5* without any visible reaction. Standing up, Andrew was tall and consumptive-looking, slightly bent. He didn't dress like an art dealer, but more like a relative of a fading landed family, a distant uncle from the country.

'I don't know, Simon, really I don't'

Simon wasn't going to help him. Andrew walked around the paintings again. A distant police car passed with a whining siren.

'Which part of yourself did you land on when you fell down that mine?' said Andrew. Again Simon gave no acknowledgement that he had even heard.

'You see, no-one's going to believe it's you. They're certainly strong. And confident. I haven't got a clue what you're trying to tell me. Did you do any of your ... previous oeuvre?'

Andrew went to look at the other new work and made an approving sigh. Then he went back to the five paintings again, and suddenly made up his mind.

'Oh dear,' he said, 'I suppose we'd better make a virtue out of necessity and tell everyone how good these are. How much were you thinking of asking for them?'

'I don't want to split them up. I'm going to do a second five. They can be ... what? Quintychs?'

'Oh no. That'll put nearly everyone off. How much for the lot?'

Simon mentioned a high figure.

'Don't be a prat,' said Andrew without a pause as he put out his cigarette in the china sink. He looked at Simon. 'Punching a bit above our weight aren't we?' he said quietly. 'That's far more than your previous best. And that was a huge painting. And rather good actually.'

He wandered around the studio in the diffused light of a beautiful morning.

'Yes, that's the way to go,' he muttered to himself. 'Instead of admitting you've freaked out, we'll say 'an exciting new direction – revolutionary change of pace – breaking new ground.' – sorry – no joke intended. We'll call it a great success, as we always do whenever we don't know what our artists are on. Success. That's the one.'

'What do you think. Yourself?'

Andrew's sigh made the cobwebs shake at the studio windows in the sunlight.

'Me? They're very confident indeed. I'd never have thought this sort of faux primitif was you, but you've pulled it off alright. You've got the vocabulary. You know what you're talking about even if we don't. They're … unsettling, which is no bad thing.' He paused for a long time. 'They're very angry,' he said at last, 'raw. like a wound.'

'That's OK isn't it?'

'Oh yes. It's OK. But will anybody buy it?' He lit another cigarette.

Before Simon could answer there was a sudden loud knocking at the door. He went down to open it and Jane flew in like a furious bird.

'Simon,' she said, rapidly climbing the stairs, 'I want to know what the fuck you think you're doing.'

'What is it this time?' said Simon, trotting up the stairs after her. 'By the way, Andrew's here, so if you wouldn't …'

'Hello Andrew,' Jane beamed. Andrew smiled uncertainly.

'Pardon me for butting in on your discussion, but I'm about to dismember your protégé. So if you don't want to witness a distressing scene …'

'Ah, Jane,' said Andrew. 'I think I'll make my way back to the hotel. I'll see you there later Simon. Lovely to see you again Jane.'

'And you, darling.'

They stood glaring at each other until Andrew had made his slow way downstairs. The door closed. They both spoke together, and then again. Then Simon said dryly, 'Ladies first.'

'You may not realise it or give a damn, Simon, but among all the other things I have to do I am trying to raise a child.'

'Yes. I know.'

'Can I finish? Thank you. I may not be the world's best mother, and I've certainly had bugger all support from anyone else, especially you, but I do my best. I do my best.'

She paused for breath. Her hennaed hair flowed to her shoulders like lava, and her clothes as usual sported colours which took no prisoners, sky-blue top, long rust-red skirt, sandals, huge silver hooped earrings. Simon still found her wildness attractive despite her murderous intent.

'So when I make an attempt to lay down the law to that stroppy little brat, I want it to mean something. I don't do it very often. But if I tell her to stay in I want her to stay in. If I give her no money, it's because I don't want her to have any bloody money. Am I making sense?'
Simon nodded, bending with the storm. It wasn't the first time or the twentieth that it had come up since they had parted, and it had been a familiar enough theme when they were together. Jane truly saw herself as the battling single parent with her chick, subverted by all around her. But she could not sustain it for long. A new circle of friends, a trip abroad, a party or two, and she would be gone. Grace was fed and housed by Simon, or relatives or friends, or later by no-one at all until Jane breezed back again, full of love and presents. She would settle down just as extremely, cook, char, spend hours of quality time bewildering to Grace, and then suddenly be off again. Grace had adored her when little, like a character from a fairy tale. But with each parting she hurt more and cared less. With adolescence had come resentment and war. Simon had been little better, happy to follow in Jane's slipstream, angry when left out. Grace was too often a chore. Too often he had let it show.

Jane was winding down. She had only come to speak not listen, so Simon confined himself to the occasional childish contradiction.

'I don't want to have to say this again, Simon. Not ever. Do you understand?'

'No.'

'Good.'

Jane turned to go, then caught sight of the new paintings for the first time.

'What the fuck are those?'

Simon said nothing.

'Are they yours?'

He nodded.

She gazed at them for a moment in silent astonishment.

'Well,' she said at last, 'at least you won't be able to bribe my daughter for much longer by the look of it. They're awful! Awful!' She whirled her hair around like a matador's cape and clumped down the stairs.

13

Simon too didn't notice the scrap of material at first. As he walked down the track a heaviness had come over him, a physical reluctance, like a force-field out of science fiction, pushing against his ambling progress. The brightness of the day seemed to ebb away. He forged on until at last he reached the clearing with the heavy sheets of plywood and the bright barbed wire.

This is where it comes from, he thought. Ground zero. Jo was right. Paintings are not enough. Thirty feet below was energy far stronger than his, a beam of light which could cut through earth, a sound which could call him through sleep, a penultimate chord hanging in the air begging for resolution. So what could he do? What difference would it make if he knew everything – who, when, why, what happened afterwards? A small aircraft buzzed overhead. Simon sat on the turf for a long time with his arms around his knees, staring at the bushes opposite.

There was no point in debating. He hadn't asked for the task but he knew it was already upon him. It was worse, more sticky than guilt. Guilt was something he could live with or shy from, duck and weave, if necessary disappear. Defiant guilt was the sea into which he had been born, the curse laid on his blonde baby head by his father's ambition, the legacy of his mother's despairing eyes, his way with all women before Jane, his standard response past or present, whether to homework undone on a schoolday morning or

Jo's gravid belly. It was a familiar evil, heavy, almost comfortable around the shoulders. This was different. He could neither argue or escape, because no-one would know. None of his usual devices would work, not petulance, coldness, vagueness, idleness, procrastination, casuistry, aggression, catatonia. Because no-one would know, but he would know, and the knowledge would never leave him alone. Someone, some person had come to this peaceful place with a child in their arms, and had left without it. Like him it had plunged into the darkness of the earth, unknown. He could never ever forget that.

He tried to put emotion aside and apply logic. It couldn't have been a stranger, a blow-in from up-country with a secret to hide. This wasn't the deed of an urban mind but someone far closer to the earth. Simon had grown up in the suburbs with new houses and straight roads and no culture to inherit, but he recognised the ways of the country. City violence had an edge. In the country things were quieter, more isolated, duller, slower, less violent, more horrible. He half-remembered a snatch of Sherlock Holmes, staring out of a train window and rebuking Dr Watson for his rosy observations on rural life. He had learned to taunt Jane with it when she waxed too romantic on the wonders of Cornwall. '... Think of the deeds of hellish cruelty, the hidden wickednesses which may go on year in, year out in such places, and none the wiser.' He shuddered. He had thought it funny once. Now it was hard in his stomach.

So it was a local. A local lady. A mother. What man or murderer would wrap the baby up warm, or ensure, oh God, that it went down holding a favourite toy. The pain rose up out of the ground like a mist, just as its echo flowed from *Painting No 5*. Raw, as Andrew had said. A wound.

And a local who lived nearby, though not too near. Not near enough to pass the spot ever again. But not a long journey either with such a burden. Someone who knew where to look, knew where secrets could be hidden. Did she ever return? Could she? Then a scrap of red caught his eye.

The schoolroom was full of tables and plastic chairs set opposite each other, as if for visiting time at an enlightened prison. Simon's table held nothing but his name on a white card. After a short but dreary wait while the occupants of the tables smiled awkwardly at each other, the first customers were trickling in. Mostly they passed Simon's table by in search of more important prey.

Terry had rung him early that morning. Terry was Head of Art, a tired dispirited drunk, clinging on by his nails to his salary and the prospect of his pension.

'Simon,' his hoarse voice had croaked, waking Simon up. He knew what to expect. Terry had the flu, or something. Clare, his number two, had four kids of her own and was fully committed, not to say stressed-out. Which left the famous part-timer, and since he was nearest, would he mind awfully covering the Year Ten Open Evening?

It was an odd sensation, being looked at searchingly by a succession of agitated parents and passed by, time after time. The whores who sit in shop windows must feel like this, he thought. When someone did finally sit down he had to jerk himself back to awareness, and struggled to remember the boy's name even after he had been told.

He located him on the register. Jack. What was his work like? His marks were middling and steady, and gave no clue. His mother looked tired and overworked, but determined to make the best of every one of her son's few talents.

'Let me think ... how can I put it ...' said Simon. Let me think, who the hell is he? Just in time a vision of a slight boy with dark hair came to mind. Liked drawing cats. He had once shown Simon a few sketches of cats playing around a sofa which were really quite good. He should have better marks than these. Terry probably didn't know who he was either. He gave a lot of middling marks just to be on the safe side.

'He's good,' said Simon. The woman's face brightened and became younger. 'But he's not at his best in class. Do you know anyone who could encourage him?'

'In what way?'

'Well, you know, some extra lessons?'

She had slumped again, and he could see her thoughts. Time, money, transport, where's it going to come from? The town was full of extravagance, galleries, high-priced restaurants, smart hotels, 4 x 4s, expensive flats and holiday homes, and hid a vast hinterland of poverty. Was Jack's dad at home? Did either of them work? If so was it probably nights at the old people's home, bar work, hairdressing, gardening, some other job at the scrag end of the pay scale. Her choices would be to buy him the football boots he needed, the swimming lessons he wanted, or get someone to help train his talent for drawing. Or just hope for the best, leaving him forever drawing cats on the backs of envelopes.

'I'll think about it. Thanks.'

She left.

After that business picked up, although his table could not match the intensity or drama of the Maths table being played out in his left ear. He could hear the repeated cycle of accusation, rebuttal and reproach, as parent after parent faced their bored children with the teacher's verdicts.

Two bodies sat down in front of him, and he was surprised to see Stacey and – presumably – her mother. Stacey was smelling of a recently extinguished cigarette and wearing too much eye make-up. She had the dog-suffering expression worn by most of the children on parade, but perked up when she saw Simon. As usual she went straight to the point.

'Oh hi Simon. Mr Ford skiving again is he?'

Simon could hardly say so.

'This is my mum.' He nodded at the plain plump woman by her side.

'Good evening Mrs Jackson.'

Stacey had talent too, a quite precocious sense of colour and dynamics, but no discipline. Her art was as slapdash and louche as the rest of her. In a different environment where there was more to look forward to she might learn to flourish, but here she seemed to Simon to be bound for a brief early flowering, followed by an eternity of steering pushchairs around the streets with a cigarette in her mouth in a gaggle of like-minded friends.

'Your marks are ... about middling.' He had a sudden urge to challenge her. 'Actually I think you're better than that Stacey. You could do very well indeed. It depends on your written work catching up with the rest.'

Mrs Jackson had sad eyes, which stared intently at Simon.

'You think?' said Stacey.

'If you work at it.'

Stacey looked thoughtful.

'OK. Thanks Simon. C'mon Mum.'

She dragged her mother off into the crowd. Mrs Jackson had looked as if there was something she had wanted to say, but just then Colin and Sally Taylor sat down with young Mark. They were both self-proclaimed artists, Sally in weaving and Colin in bleak sculptures of local granite. They claimed immediate kinship with Simon, artists to artist. From the way they lowered themselves down Simon could see that they intended to stay for a while.

At the other end of town the crush was getting thicker in the Mermaid. The holiday season had crept up on the town without ceremony and suddenly it was full of strangers. Jo and Nadia struggled out into the beer garden with their drinks, shouting at each other to be heard. An Irish band were diddling through a loud, bad PA by the bar.

'I'd better not have any more after this,' shouted Jo.

'Adding units?' replied Nadia,' It's only vodka. Vodka doesn't count.'

They leaned over a low balcony side by side, looking at the sea.

'I couldn't do this at home,' said Nadia, 'It's still freezing in London. I love the way the night air's so soft already. It's busy too isn't it?'

It was. The streets of most of the more staid Cornish holiday towns were deserted by this hour, but in front of them the harbour road was flooded with young, noisy people for whom the night was just beginning.

'I think we're being watched,' said Jo as quietly as she could. She pointed with a finger concealed at her waist. Nadia followed the gesture and noticed two young men staring down the garden at them. They really were young, barely into their twenties, crop-headed, and keen-looking. You could almost see the aftershave, Jo thought. One wore a coloured T-shirt over jeans, the other light trousers and a football top.

'Let's give them the stare back,' said Nadia, and they both giggled. The vodka had warmed Jo right through to her legs, even to the lump of ice in her stomach which had been her companion since the night at the mine. Slowly they both turned together and stared at the boys, from top slowly to bottom and back up again, then turned away, doubling up like teenagers.

'God, I haven't done that for ages,' said Jo. 'Christ, it's good to laugh.'

'Simon wasn't really a bag of laughs, was he?'

Jo hadn't thought about him all evening.

'No. Too far up himself. He could be funny if he wanted to, but ...'

'You two live around here then?'

They'd already forgotten the boys, but the appraisal hadn't gone unnoticed, and they had plucked up their Dutch courage and moved in. They were standing so close that Jo couldn't fail to realise how right she had been.

'Why?'

'We're strangers round here. We thought you could show us around.'

'Yeah. Show us the way, like.' said the other.

'The way out's over there,' said Nadia.

'Don't be like that,' said the first. 'We heard that the natives were friendly.'

'Only if they're treated right,' said Nadia, with a huge wink at Jo. Christ, thought Jo, she's only bloody flirting with them. A flood of memories from school came back to her. In her mood, Nadia would say anything, do anything, take any dare. So often Jo had slipstreamed behind her with her heart in her mouth, but Nadia had always got away with it.

'Fancy another drink?' said the one in the football shirt.

'We're alright thanks,' said Jo, feeling old.

The T-shirt was called Dave and the footy shirt Daniel. They were down from Reading. They worked in marketing. They'd never been to Cornwall before, always Spain or Italy or Ibiza. Cornwall was nice, quaint, cute. They'd tried surfing at Sennen. Dave had managed to get up once – pause for laughter – Daniel had been rubbish at it. They were quite sweet, if very young and quite stupid. Time passed. Another round of drinks arrived, although Jo couldn't remember ordering any. Dave finally said, 'Shall we go somewhere else?'

'OK,' said Nadia, straight away. In seconds they were out on the seafront. Dave and Dan had obviously sorted matters out in the gents, and Dave closed in on Jo while Daniel drew alongside Nadia. Jo felt Dave's lean arm go around her waist. She caught

Nadia's eyes, which were sparkling with mischief. The ball was rolling. What was she thinking? Surely she wasn't going to take them home? Dave held her tightly, although he obviously couldn't think of anything to say.

The seafront was busy. Out of the crowd came a trio of girls. In the middle Jo recognised the black clothes and pale form of Grace. As they were about to pass Grace saw them in turn. She did a visible double take, and then her lip curled in disbelief.

'Hi Jo,' she said. She stared again, then started to move off with her friends. 'Bloody hell ...' Jo heard her say in a wondering voice as she passed on.

Suddenly Jo saw herself through Grace's eyes, and a basin of cold water fell over her. She closed her eyes for a minute and stopped dead. As the chill passed off she felt suddenly, urgently sick.

'You alright?' said Dave, his grip slackening a little.
Nadia looked at her. 'You OK Jo?' she said.

'No ...'
She shook off Dave's arm and ran down a set of granite steps leading to the wet sand of the empty harbour. In the shadow of the wall she bent over and vomited into a pool, while the salt water seeped through the sand into her shoes. Nadia appeared beside her, but said nothing until she had finished. Nadia passed her a tissue.

'Get rid of them, Nady.'

The boys, whose blood was still up, were coming down the steps. Vomiting girls were nothing amiss to veterans of Ibiza.

'Sorry boys, sod off.'

'Nah, she'll be alright. Come back to our flat and have some coffee.'

'Take no for an answer.'

'Oh leave it out. We're having fun. We like you two,' said Dave, attempting to get close to Jo once more.

'You do, do you?' said Nadia, 'Well perhaps I'd better tell you now that she's pregnant and I'm a lesbian. OK?'

The boys looked at each other for a moment.

'OK. C'mon Dan,' said Dave with a sigh. There was still time to get back to the pub. Their shapes disappeared from the top of the steps. Nadia went up to check that all was clear, and Jo tottered up the steps, feeling better. They sat in silence in the taxi on the way back.

As they were sitting over coffee back at the cottage, Jo suddenly said, 'Are you?'

'I knew you were going to ask that!' cackled Nadia, and her face wrinkled up in an evil smile. 'Gissa kiss!'

' ... sod off, you poof ...'

As if. But then, anything could happen. She really was pregnant.

14

Ti rang the cottage just as Jo was coming out of the shower the next morning. Jo had a slight hangover, and just the usual nausea. Her memories of the previous night were cartoon-like, funny, embarrassing. Nadia was fast asleep.

'Just to let you know, darling. We put Simon's new ... pictures up last night.'
There was a pause. Jo said nothing.
'Just so you won't have a ... shock.'
'Why. Are they good?'
Oh God, she hadn't meant to say that. Ti's pause was, for once, quite genuine as she decided how best to avoid the implication.
'Yes ... they are. They're quite ... powerful too. And big. It took us all evening to get them up. I had to send Richard home for his Black and Decker at one point.'
'Really? Wow.'
'Yes. Now, the photographer from *Cornwall Daily* is coming round at about midday. I should be back, but keep him talking if I'm not. I want to make sure he gets the pictures in the right order and does them justice for once. It just won't do to have them postage stamp sized.'
Water was dripping down Jo's front, making her shiver. Outside it was raining hard.
'So glad we got them in before the ... weather changed.'
Jo wondered how Ti could even make small talk about the weather

sound like an aesthetic judgement.

'OK,' she said, 'I'm on my way in.'

She put down the phone and towelled her hair furiously. Shouting a curt goodbye at Nadia, she ran to the car and drove angrily through the rain. At the gallery she fumbled damply for the key, and stepped into the church-like gloom inside.

The paintings stretched away, a pattern of indistinct shapes and colours, totally unexpected and confusing. The last one contained an image which reminded her of the pregnancy book she had been reading in the library. A foetus – surely he wouldn't use that? Not even Simon. Even artists have places they don't tread, don't they? It occurred to her that she didn't know Simon very well. She noticed the concealed red and yellow smiles. Was he laughing at her? She stared for a moment, then turned on the banks of halogen spotlights. The colours jumped off the wall, so strongly that she gasped. She ran her eyes along the line again. The passion and anger beat on her eyes. Christ. What was he saying? She felt sick, and sank down onto a seat. What the hell was he saying? And why didn't he say it to her face?

She found herself in tears, and quickly switched the lights off again. She was in no shape to open up shop. Luckily her desk faced across the width of the shop not its length, so she wouldn't have to stare at them all day. What was eating him? Why couldn't he talk about it? She went into the tiny kitchen and poured out a cup of water. Sipping it, she made herself turn the lights back on and go down the line once more.

She missed him. She was cultivating her memory of his anger, selfishness, deviousness, but had forgotten his passion. She wanted that back again. She was almost calm. She turned round the Celtic-lettered 'Open' sign and put some soothing music on. Thanks Simon. Heartbreak, heartburn, hangover. And now this.

Ti and the photographer arrived at the same time. A technical discussion followed. There was no way of including all five pictures, and no chance of enough space in the paper to show them all. They would have to choose one. Ti pointed wordlessly at *No 5*, and the photographer began to set up. When Simon arrived, they grabbed him. He gave Jo a winning smile and said 'Hi ...', then succumbed to the grooming process as the other two fussed around him, making him try various poses. Jo took an early lunch, and when she came back Simon had gone, leaving no message.

Early in the afternoon she went out again. It was her first mandatory pre-abortion counselling session. Due to holidays, sickness, recruitment problems, etc, etc, the counsellor was a man, which made her angry straight away, partly because Nadia had bet her that it would be. Not a young man either, probably an old gynaecologist called back from retirement. The counsellor took her anger for nerves and tried in his patronising way to soothe her, with the opposite effect. Yes, she'd had a chance to think about it, and no, she'd never had a baby before, and yes oh yes, the relationship had irretrievably broken down. The man made a reference to Simon's rights, to which Jo listened in a cold silence. How had she come to be pregnant? The usual way. Ask Simon, she answered. He knew she was not on the pill. All the pills she'd ever tried had made her feel awful and put her off sex altogether. Anyway, she said, getting into her stride and quoting Nadia, why should she screw up the whole of her body with hormones when a man could slip a contraceptive on and off like a lollipop-wrapper without any ill-effects? Quite, quite. Was she absolutely sure she wished to go ahead with the termination? Yes, quite sure. He was already writing her notes before she answered. Another girl was waiting in the corridor when she stamped out. Busy, busy. It was quickly done, but she still slipped into the pub for a subversive brandy before going back to where Simon's incoherent message was screaming at her from the walls.

Nadia could work from her lap-top for a couple of days, reviewing albums and gigs by bands she didn't like, but she had to go back to London before she was missed. She looked Jo in the eyes for a long time.

'Don't worry about me,' Jo said.

'Sure, sure,' said Nadia. 'You're fine here, with your absent shit of a boyfriend, abortion coming up, weirdos queuing in the garden. Why don't you come up with me for a bit? Have your abortion in civilisation.'

'I'm OK.'

Nadia looked at her deeply once more then gave her a quick hug.

'Right,' she said, 'I'm off. Take good care.'

Simon picked up *Cornwall Daily* after lunch, but was too busy finishing off other paintings to give it attention until he was back at the flat. Suddenly tired, he ate a plate of pasta and carefully read the article. Next to it was a photograph of him looking suitably solemn beside *Picture No 5*. The article was more or less right, except the teeth-grating word 'promising' which had cursed so much of his publicity. After eating he put his head down onto the table for a moment, hoping his mind would clear.

Jo. Why couldn't he ring her? It was out of his control, just when it should all have started to sing. He started a few imaginary conversations, each of which ended in a cowardly row. He watched a film and went to bed early. No-one rang.

He woke up in the darkness, wide-awake, covered in sweat, fumbling for the light. The toad! The bloody toad. He'd been alright until the toad. He could still feel its cold weight on his bare foot. He shook his head to shake the vision out. He picked up the paper which he had dropped by the bed. This time when he scanned the photograph it was not the expression on his own face which took his attention. It was the shape at the edge of the painting, still unnamed, still unmourned. Portrait of the artist smouldering quietly towards the camera, while in the ground was a loose human end which would not lie down. Somewhere it had had a name, and a home, and a mother. And a father too, another cold-hearted bastard in denial probably, just like him. Who must share his secret. Were they awake tonight too? Probably no more than a couple of miles away. He switched on the radio to drown the noises in his head.

The woman wasn't the average gallery customer. She was obviously local, middle-aged and plump, dressed in an old brown coat, with a fawn umbrella against the rain. In her hand was the newspaper, folded over to Simon's picture. Jo took a telephone call from Richard about another photographer from a monthly who wanted an appointment. When she got off the phone the woman was still there. She was very still, staring at *Painting No 5*. Tamsin, a silver jeweller, dropped in with a few extra ear-rings and stayed for a few minutes. She left, but the woman had not moved. Jo could see a little of her face. It was big and plain and defeated-looking, but changing, twisted with pain which was still welling up, stretching it out of shape. Something about her seemed to stir in Jo's memory, but it was too deep to grasp.

'Can I help you?' Jo said gently. To her distress the woman gave a bursting sob and rushed past Jo and out of the door.

Ti passed her in the doorway. She was too well-bred to say anything but fixed Jo with a puzzled enquiring look as she came in.

'I don't know,' said Jo in answer to the look. 'She just stood there in front of Simon's pictures for a few minutes and then went rushing out, very upset.'

Ti continued to stare in her unsettling way.

'Perhaps she was a critic,' said Jo.

Ti's face finally softened to something approaching a smile. 'Now

now,' she said, 'One may find Simon's new work ... challenging, but it shouldn't cause people to ... flee.'

'No,' said Jo. 'The usual reaction so far is silence. And stillness. People really can't work them out.'

'But they respond,' said Ti with something approaching emotion, 'that is what distinguishes Simon from other ... equally talented ... artists. His pictures can't be glanced at in passing. They demand your attention.'

Yes, thought Jo. Attention seeking, to put it another way. The artist was true to himself.

'What do you think of them? You haven't really said and you are usually fairly ... forthright in your views.'

'I think they're amazing.'

Ti unconsciously straightened a piece of silver jewellry in a display case with her delicate fingers.

'But ...?'

'But they're like a message from another planet. A loud one. One I can't understand. I find them a bit panicky to tell the truth.'

Ti looked at her with a kindly expression, making it clear that she was making allowances for the repressed passion of a troubled love affair, yet without judging it.

'So important that we all see with different eyes ... '

15

Half a mile over the stony moors from Jo's cottage was the main farm complex of Menwartha. Many years before during a brief enthusiasm for the outdoors Simon and Jane had gone to explore its sole claim to fame, a large single Neolithic standing-stone in a meadow close to the farm. He remembered it quite clearly, partly because the farmer was renowned for his dislike for visitors. All the paths were deep in mud, and a pack of pale-eyed collies barked incessantly in the yard. It was raining then too – perhaps it had been their last ever expedition, the one which had convinced them to give up ancient mysteries altogether in favour of something more hedonistic. He remembered the broken roofs of the sheds and the flapping corrugated iron, the rusting machinery left in the open, the smell of sour silage, the roar of the farmer's voice inside the milking shed and the noisy whack of his stick. The stone too was singularly lacking in magic, standing in a small pool of muddy water, smeared with muck and hair from the cows who had rubbed against it. They must have walked past Jo's cottage on the way back, Simon suddenly realised, although he didn't remember it. It was a long time ago, but it was the nearest farm to the mine shaft, and he had to start somewhere.

At home that morning he had stretched out his new large scale map of the area over the dining table and studied it carefully. The shaft was marked, though it took him a while to find it amongst the other unfamiliar signage, the contour lines, field shapes, farmsteads and lanes. He marked it with a red dot and took out the old school compass he sometimes used for making formal circles. Sticking the point into the red mark, he drew a few concentric circles in faint pencil. The Brigadier would have been proud of him. He even remembered some of the soldier's jargon from walks long ago; knolls, spinneys, promontories, dead ground. Here they all were if he could only understand them.

But dwellings were few. The complex of Menwartha stood out, a large hilltop farm of unknown history. Here was Jo's cottage on its own. Two or three pre-war bungalows stood on the lower slopes, with a field or two each. Bosmergy farm and cottage. The possible remnants of a stone circle. He increased the radius. Winnard farm. An ancient wind pump. The corner of a footpath. A row of three or four cottages, and close by the small quarry they had once served. A mine chimney, now ruined. That was all.

The lane wended through bracken and gorse, showing signs of recent mending. Simon bent his head against the drizzle and followed it. Near the buildings it turned into smooth tarmac. An open gate led into the middle of the granite buildings, and Simon looked around in despair. The sordid bleakness of ages had gone from Menwartha, but so too had everything else.

The sheds he remembered had all disappeared, the corrugated iron Dutch barn and the asbestos-roofed cowsheds. The black plastic silage clamp with its evil puddles had gone, although the ramp from which slurry was once pushed into a waiting spreader had been preserved, perhaps as some kind of knowing joke. The granite buildings were all immaculately re-roofed with dark slates and bright orange ridge tiles, fitted with small pane windows and stained wood doors. Every granite barn was now a dwelling. The space between them was gravelled, and at their sides were laid out gardens that even Simon knew would never grow anything. New hedges and private gates surrounded him, and the only echo of the farm's previous incarnation were a couple of dogs, a spaniel and a Labrador, barking at each other as much as at him from their separate enclosures. A shiny 4 x 4 was parked outside one former barn, but there seemed to be no-one there. The original farmhouse was closed up, thick faded curtains blinding its windows. A new sign pointed the path to the standing stone and a tidy stile had appeared in the hedge to lead the way.

He endured the barking dogs for five minutes, but no-one came out. He was just leaving when a stout elderly man appeared at an upstairs window of one of the barn conversions.

'Looking for someone?' he shouted.

'No,' Simon replied, 'I don't think so. Do any of the old families still live here?'

The man rubbed his jowls. 'Don't think so,' he replied, 'the farmhouse is a holiday let. These two over here only come down in the summer. She over there works in Truro, but she's only renting. The cottage people are in Cyprus for a month. That just leaves me, and I've only been here for, let me see, um, six years? Yes it must be. Marvellous place for short wave radio. Ever tried it? Better than the internet …'

'No,' said Simon. 'I don't suppose you know what happened to them?'

The man pondered. The complex was the highest point around and a chill wind blew through the empty farmyard, making Simon wrap his coat around himself more tightly.

'Retired I suppose. The old man never once came back, so they said, after he'd gone. I think he's dead now. The grandchildren used to come back and hang around but I haven't seen any of them for years. You look cold. Have you come to look at the stone? You must be one of the first this year …'

'No, no. I've seen it. I was more interested in what had become of the farm.'

'Would you like a cup of tea? I was about to take a break …'

'No thanks,' said Simon. 'I was just being curious.'

'Try the pub,' said the man. 'They'll know.'

Half an hour later Simon ducked his head into the doorway of the Duke of Cornwall. It was high up on the moors attached to a small hamlet, once the hub of a circle of miners and farm labourers, but now almost deserted. Somehow the pub had survived the emptying of the countryside and the breathalyser, and now made a passable living from walkers, family lunches, and occasional live music. But the landlords had been wise enough to keep a small, dingy public bar for the old men who hated change. A coal fire glowed in the open fireplace, and six or seven locals were hunched around a table playing or watching a game of euchre.

As Simon came in, all sound ceased for a moment. Identifying him from his waterproofs as a walker the old men lost interest at once and resumed their game. He ordered a drink and sat quietly, wondering how to begin, but in the end the job was done for him. On the way to the bar one of the card school looked more closely at Simon.

'Been down any more mine shafts lately?' he asked. The table turned and stared at him all together without embarrassment.

'How did you manage it?'

'Lost his balance trying to paint a picture, most likely,' said a man with bushy white eyebrows. Simon started, but then remembered *Cornwall Daily*. The old boys didn't miss much.

'My dog got lost. I was looking for him.'

'Ah.'

Simon followed up. 'Who owns that mine? Does anybody know?'

The discussion that followed was lively and prolonged, and Simon found himself forgotten in the process. The question of who owned a mine was no simple matter. He hadn't realised that one grandee might have owned the land, another the mineral rights, and another the franchise to mine the ground. He in turn might subcontract the actual work to a mine captain, who chose those who finally broke sweat and pitted their bodies against the native rock. After several minutes of admittedly fascinating lore about extinct companies and their links with local landowners, he decided to take the reins once more.

'Whose is the land around there?'

'Hm,' said an old man with a pipe, 'that land went back to Lord Porthtowan some while back, didn't it Tom?'

'Who farmed it before?'

'Before?' said the old man. 'That would have been Cyril Stevens. He had Menwartha for donkey's years.'

The others agreed.

'Does anyone farm around here now?'

'Winnard,' said Tom. 'Winnard's still milking. That's the only one now. All the rest are gone.'

'I used to work at Menwartha,' started another, 'and there were six other farms on this hillside sending milk over to the dairy. Yes … six. Must have been couple of dozen of men working. We had seven men up Menwartha …'

'Why did the land go back to Lord Porthtowan?'

'You an estate agent? Or thinking of suing someone for falling down that mine?'

White-eyebrows' voice was like a shower of cold water. The others drew back and looked at Simon afresh.

'No,' said Simon. 'It was my own stupid fault.' They still looked guarded. 'I haven't been up to Menwartha for ages,' he went on, 'The farm's changed a bit hasn't it?'

The slow hubbub broke out again. 'There's nothing in farming these days … see what they paid for those barns … used to be a strong farm once ...'

'So what happened to Cyril Stevens then?'

'Dead. There was no-one to follow him, so it was took back in hand. Happens all the time.'

'No kids?'

There was a pause, as they spent a moment with their memories.

'Son,' said the man with the pipe. 'Nice lad. Moved over to America years ago.'

There was another pause.

'No-one else?' said Simon, as lightly as he could.

The card school looked at each other.

'Cyril had a daughter didn't he?'

'That's right. She married a schoolteacher and moved away.' said a man in a shirt and tie who hadn't spoken before.

'What about Bosmergy?' Simon remembered. The group went quiet.

'Willie Richards's place,' said Tom. 'He's gone too. Still living though. Must be getting on a bit,' he added, without irony.

'He's in the same home as my cousin Queenie,' said white-eyebrows.

'Is his family still up there?'

'No. He had a couple of girls and a son. Died in the Falklands, the boy.'

They all fell silent again, in memoriam.

'What you want to know for?' said the man in the shirt and tie, suddenly hard.

Simon ploughed fluently on, 'I'm thinking of doing a series of paintings of farming as it used to be, before it's all forgotten. I'm looking to see what families are still around, that's all.'

He regretted his slick words several times in the next half-hour. The card school had all worked on the land in one way or another and all had tales to tell of cattle, horses, favourite bits of machinery, storms, droughts and hardships of every sort. One by one their glasses emptied and sat in a line on the table. The message finally got through and Simon bought another round. The conversation flowed even more freely.

He drew the discussion gradually back to Cyril Stevens's daughter.

'Where did she go to after she married?' No-one knew and a

silence fell.

'Bristol,' said the woman who had come to clear the empty glasses away. 'Got three kids. Eldest must be in university by now.' Simon turned to her.

'What was she called?'

'Annie. Went to school with me.'

'What's her surname now?'

Simon felt he was pushing his luck, but the woman seemed happy to oblige.

'Cald ... Calderfield, that's it. Sends me a card every Christmas. She's doing very well. Works in a bank.'

Stop, said Simon to himself. He had been about to ask which bank, but realised that the art of detective work might lie in not making your objective too obvious. He wound the conversation down, spread a few good wishes around the euchre school and emerged blinking into the grey afternoon.

A few miles away a wiry man stared aggressively at a plump middle-aged woman who was bending forward over a kitchen table, weeping.

'Brenda will you shut up!' said Gary. 'Stop all that crying for Christ's sake. I don't need it.'

'I'm sorry,' said the woman opposite him, 'I can't help it. I don't know what to do.'

'I get back from sea knackered out, looking forward to a rest and what do I get? Tears, fuss. Hassle. Pull yourself together.'

From upstairs the sound of loud music echoed through the terraced house, fast guitars and roaring voices.

'He knows ...' she wept.

'He don't know shit. That was all years ago.'

'But he was down the shaft. And then that picture ...'

Gary picked up *Cornwall Daily* again.

'Could be anything. You don't know nothing about art. They sit in front of anything from a bowl of fruit to a naked woman and paint the same fucking thing. A kid of three could have done it.'

'I knew this would happen.'

'Nothing's happened! It's just a coincidence. Think about something else. Cheer up.'

'It isn't. He knows. I know he does. He saw something down there. And now it's all going to come out.'

There was a moment's silence before the next track, broken only by Brenda's sobs.

'Look,' said Gary, 'if he'd seen something he'd have told someone, right. The police, right? You'd have heard if they'd found anything. He wouldn't find … that, and then run home and do a bloody painting would he? Nobody would. I mean what's the fucking sense in that? Anyway,' he went on, 'it wasn't your fault. You told me that often enough.'

'Yes it was. It'll all come out,' wept Brenda. 'All of it. Everyone will know. I couldn't bear it.'

'Cut it out Brenda or I'll give you a bloody slap, see if I don't. It's all in your imagination. You ought to …' he suddenly broke off, jumped up from his chair and strode into the hall.

'Oy,' he shouted up the stairs, 'turn that fucking row down! Did you hear me?' The noise continued unabated. 'I said, "Turn it down!" Stacey! Did you hear me?'

16

Simon walked slowly back to the car, thinking about the women who were normally too old and plain to attract his notice. There was a whole swathe of women who, because of their age and size, he didn't really see. They were the school dinner ladies, some of the parents. They had short unmemorably tidy hair, roundish faces with little make-up, unfashionable clothes, no waists or other indications of shape, serviceable shoes, handbags. Mostly they talked only to other, similar women. They rarely raised their voices or did anything else to draw attention to themselves.

Simon felt a twinge of shame. There were thousands, hundreds of thousands of them if he thought about it. Decent, worthwhile people, like his own Aunt Jean in Torquay. Invisible. What do you say to them? How do you start a conversation, especially one which starts with bland chatter and ends with questions which might flay the skin off their backs? He started to walk again. Really, clearly, it would be best to forget the whole thing, or learn to cope with it, or spill it out to some anonymous counsellor, or in some other way spit it out of his mind, get over it, and get on with his life.

He thought longingly once more of the police. They had the experience and resources, they could lift a phone, send a well-trained, concerned officer to an address in Bristol that afternoon, ask a few formal questions which the woman would be too frightened not to answer, and the whole thing would move swiftly to a conclusion. To closure. It would be so easy.

But he couldn't let it go. They had been too long together that night in the dark. The bony fingers had reached out to him alone, the hidden eyes had met his with their appeal. If there was any reason in anything it was that he should have been the one to fall, and to find. There was more to it than police action could achieve. What closure, when the veils were ripped away and the sad and dreadful forces behind the crime were served up like a steak on the jaded forks of the media? The child had slipped under Simon's shield which held the rest of humanity so successfully at a distance, and become his own. It was his journey, he thought as the second pint of beer warmed his brain and filled him with sentiment. His quest.

The Brigadier would have known what to do. He would have had a plan, an objective, no nonsense. Life was a simple matter to him of motive and action, with no self-questioning in between. If he wanted something he went for it, a job, a house, a woman, whatever. He would have found Simon's quest baffling, just as everything about Simon left him baffled. His mother would have let sleeping dogs lie. If only they would.

He arrived at the car and pulled off his wet waterproofs. He drove slowly back to the flat, almost unaware of what he was doing. What next?

There were newspaper archives, parish registers and other records. But if the child had been on record it would have been laid somewhere fitting, not just dropped out of sight. Where were dark secrets like that recorded, except in the memory of those involved? His answerphone was flashing. He knew it would be Jo. He turned it off without listening.

He looked out of the window for half an hour, and then reluctantly pulled a directory out from behind the sofa. There was only one way.

Simon stepped out gratefully into the echoing space of Temple Meads station. It was great to be away. Cornwall was a subtle addiction, full of reasons for ease and delay, cradling in its familiarity. In winter his face was known to more than half the population, some who greeted him and many more who did not. Nevertheless they noticed his passing, knew who he was, where he lived, who he walked around with. Or if that was not true it seemed to be, which amounted to the same thing. To be unknown was to be free, loose in the undergrowth again.

He took a bus to the town centre and paused outside the first bank he encountered. It was bigger than he had expected, with surely too many employees tucked behind the smoked glass or up the executive stairs for any to know all the others. He went through the automatic door and gazed at the line of counter assistants.

Impossible. Crazy, and better to stop now. The next step crossed the line. He would be remembered for his enquiries. If the chain of circumstances ever did involve the police, they could reverse the process with ease and arrive where he stood now, teetering on the brink. A man asking for Annie Calderfield. About five-foot-nine, thirty – thirty-five, fair hair. Seemed nervous.

He looked again at the smart girls behind the counters. Too young, all of them. But of course. They would always put the young and pretty ones to the fore, to attract men like him. He stood quite still and a shine of sweat appeared at his temples, like condensation on a cold window.

'Can I help you at all?'

He jumped visibly as the woman in the corporate uniform presented herself before him with a professional smile.

'Yes. I'm looking for someone. An old friend. We've lost touch but I think she works here.'

The smile turned to a frown.

'I'm sorry but we're not allowed to give out any information about our personnel. You know, security…'

'I understand,' said Simon, enjoying lying as he always did once he was in the swing of it. 'But if she does work here I was wondering if you could give her my mobile number so she could ring me?'

'Well …'

'Have you worked here long?' said Simon, to distract her.

She was smiling again. 'Oh yes. Ten or eleven years. Of course it's all changed a lot in that time …' He let her run on. She slowed to a stop, assessed once more whether Simon was any kind of a business prospect, decided he was not, and paused to enjoy his good looks for a moment before making up her mind.

'What's her name?'

'Annie Calderfield.'

'Annie Calderfield.'

'Never 'eard of her.'

The young man was thin and tall, with jelled black hair. He was also rude and rather stupid, Simon thought. By now he had a perspective on bank employees, having interviewed eight of them. The boy opposite him had insisted he sit down, and had pressed details of mortgages and insurance into his hand. He wasn't really listening to what Simon said. Instead his mind was full of contacts and targets and the car he was desperate to win.

'Write it down please,' said Simon with petulant authority. 'And my number. These rates on the introductory offer look quite tasty by the way,' he went on, knowing as ever which buttons to press. 'I'll have a look at them tonight and probably get back to you tomorrow.'

The boy looked up with foxy eyes.

'How d'ya spell it?'

At last, exhausted, he retreated as the banks closed, had supper and sat reading in the room of his guest-house, occasionally checking his mobile to see that it was receiving properly. It was, but it did not ring.

The next morning he sought the smaller branches in the inner circle around the city centre. These were more difficult as they were more intimate, and the staff had time to chat and ask nosey questions of their own. His cover story grew and flourished – how they knew each other – how they had lost touch – why he wanted to meet again. It had all the cheap resonance of a TV soap, and some of the women who heard it gave him piercing looks to show that they understood there was more to tell, perhaps a secret heartbreak, a love denied. But none of them knew Annie, though many obviously wished they did.

In the afternoon he gave up and went to the cinema, although he kept his telephone on. He had paid for two nights, so he went back again in the evening to the wallpapered room with its thin walls and plastic ensuite.

He was just about to turn on the 10 o'clock news on the tiny television suspended above his bed when his mobile rang.
    'Hello.'
    'Who is this please?'
    'Simon White. Is that Annie Calderfield?'
    'Who are you?'
Her voice showed no sign of a Cornish accent. It was clipped and professional, tinged with suspicion and annoyance.
    'I was given your name by the lady in the Duke of Cornwall,' said Simon quickly. Christ, what was her name, the chatty woman behind the bar? 'June,' he remembered just in time.
    'What do you want me for?'

There was no softening of the tone. It was perhaps even sharper. He decided to stick as closely to the truth as possible.

'I'm doing a sort of project on Menwartha Farm. I'm an artist, and very interested in local history.' She remained silent, letting him talk, while the thinness of his story stuck his lips together. He ground to a halt.

'If you're that interested,' she replied with logic, 'I don't see why you don't ask around down there instead of coming up here and chasing after me. Anyway I've nothing to say. I grew up there and that's it.'

'It's changed a lot since then.'

'I dare say it has, but I couldn't care less.'

'It's just that I want to go back to when it was a proper working farm, seen as you saw it, through the eyes of a child. No-one else could know it in the way you did. Do you see what I mean?'

'Not really.'

But she was lowering her guard.

'It's hard to explain. I'm not Cornish, I didn't grow up there. I need to talk to someone who did. No-one else will talk to me.'

'Well that's no surprise ...'

'Look I don't want to badger you. Could we meet for a coffee or something tomorrow?'

'Well I don't really ...'

'Please. Ten minutes would be fine ...' There was a vexed pause.

'Oh I suppose so. Since you've gone to so much trouble to find me.'

'Jo could you pop in here for a minute.' Ti's tone was as even as ever, and Jo went into the tiny office thinking of ten other things.

'Yes?'

'Sit down for a moment.'

She sat down. Ti held a pause which was even for her something of a record, while Jo's stomach went slowly down a lift.

'Is something the matter?' Ti said at last.

This was terra incognita. In the usual way Ti would no more ask after her welfare than give her a full body hug. Ti also was clearly feeling the awkwardness of the situation and gave a small smile, which was as close as she could get to embarrassed fellow feeling. Jo could only play for time.

'Why?'

'You seem … distracted. And lately … not your usual cheerful self.'

'I'm sorry,' said Jo, more defensively than she intended. 'I'll make an effort to cheer up. Perhaps spring's been a little slow this year. I must be short of sunlight.'

Her bravado petered out, while Ti's gaze never slackened.

'Simon is something of a … sandy foundation to build upon,' she said finally.

Jo felt the blush warming up beneath her ears and bit back the urge to swear in Ti's cultured face. However looking into her eyes she discerned a ghost of the warmth she kept hidden from the world. She remembered some gossip; Ti's whirlwind union with Richard late in life, even some talk of a miscarriage … She was a woman after all, Jo realised, although it was difficult to think of her as a sister under the skin.

'I know,' she said finally.

'I see him as something of … an Easter egg,' Ti said unexpectedly. She didn't have to explain. The glitter, the sweet skin, then … maybe nothing at all in the secret darkness.

'Do you like him?' said Jo.

Ti reeled slightly at such a direct question. 'I like him better than Richard does,' she mused. 'He always describes him as … forgive me, something I wouldn't care to repeat.'

'Try me. I probably agree.'

'… a slippery bastard.'

Jo wanted to laugh, hearing such a crudity emerge from the

delicate lips. She also had a terrible counter-urge to pull herself up to her full height and say 'Do you realise you are referring to the father of my child?'

'But yes of course I like him,' Ti went on. 'He is charming, nice-looking, can be funny. Clever too. But, you know, not my ... cup of tea.'

Richard was her cup of tea, then. He was straightforward, down to earth, unpretentious, and worshipping the ground she walked on. And Richard could never in a million years be Jo's cup of tea, so she smiled, somehow on equal terms again.

'I hate to think of you ... eating yourself up ... over him.'

'It's the bloody pictures!' said Jo, astonished at her own outburst. 'I have to look at them all day. They really disturb me. I don't know what he's saying, but it's like someone shouting a warning outside the door, in a foreign language, who won't shut up but won't tell you what the trouble is. Don't you feel like that?'

'They are ... powerful. Quite a surprise.'

'I can cope with Simon. I'm not a child. But the pictures just get under my skin.'

'Is that really all?' Her lambent gaze was on Jo's face, making her want to cry, confess.

'Yes. Really.'

Ti sighed gently. 'Take three or four days off,' she said, 'Go and ... sort him out.'

Jo smiled again at her sudden directness. 'Thank you,' she said quietly.

Annie sent Simon a text, saying her coffee breaks were short and lunch would be easier, even mentioning a café. He smiled ruefully. At least the bush telegraph must have given him a reasonable press when she checked him out overnight with whatever Cornish connections she still had back home.

Her dark hair was beginning to be flecked with grey, but she seemed younger than her years. She walked into the café with vitality and sat down next to him with easy confidence, emphasised by her business suit. He liked her immediately. She made no pretence about the results of her overnight research, made a few flattering remarks about his success, and relaxed her guard. They went through the formalities of ordering, then sat back.

'Why Menwartha in particular?'

'I walked through there years ago, and again just last week. You wouldn't know it was the same place.'

'Everyone tells me how nice and tidy it is now.'

Simon elaborated fluently, telling Annie how the fate of farms like Menwartha was changing the nature of the county, how clean and clinical the countryside was becoming, and how very soon there would be almost nothing left to remember it by. He spoke of his urge to capture that, the reality of toil and make-do, the dour daily struggle, the physical effort by which people were once fed. By the time he finished he was so impassioned that he really did want to paint it.

Annie was impressed. As the food arrived she opened up and talked about the life of a farmer's girl, from letting the hens in and out to getting the calves to drink from a bucket, to her least favourite, picking the early flowers in February and March. Simon's questions gently probed her relationship with her father, but she was uncomplicated on the subject.

'Yes, he was a bad tempered old devil, as everybody knows. But he spoiled me rotten. No-one knows how kind he could be, and he'd hate it if I told you.' she laughed, with a kindly open air laugh.

'Really? He gave me a good shouting at.'

'His bark was a lot worse than his bite. People like you just see farmers as they go by. You don't see them getting up early seven days a week, working 'til late, coping with all weathers, looking after animals with all that can go wrong with them, trying to make it all pay. He had a hard old life. You probably caught him on a bad day.'

'You must miss him.'

'I do. I hoped he'd have a nice long retirement and give himself a bit of a rest, but he didn't last long. Most farmers are like that. It's the work that keeps them going, and once it stops, they stop too. I think about him every day.'

She paused for a minute and stared unseeingly at the table. Simon's stomach started to knot. Time was getting on.

'Did you hear about my mishap in the mine?'

'Yes, someone mentioned it. How on earth did you manage that?' she said, with eyes twinkling over her coffee-cup.

He paused, feeling the sweat break out on his palms.

'When I was down there ... I found something.'

The smile left her eyes.

'What?'

'I wondered ... if you might be able to guess?'

'Don't think so.'

He said nothing. She looked at him, staring, as if seeing him for the first time. The woman at the next table suddenly laughed, but neither of them looked away.

'What?' she said again. 'Why are you looking at me like that? What was down there?'

Then her eyes closed hard in pain, as if a migraine had dropped its weight upon her, got up suddenly from the table and walked towards the door. Simon thought she was leaving, but she disappeared into the toilet.

Simon paid the bill and waited for a long time. Another woman went into the toilet and came out, giving Simon an odd glance as she went. Finally Annie came briskly out again into the world.

'That's what all this was for I suppose,' she said in a tight voice.

'Come and sit down.'

'No, I'm going. I'll be late for work. Thank you for lunch.'
She went for the door, and Simon could not stop her. But he kept alongside her on the pavement.

'I have to know, that's all.'

'No, you don't,' she snapped. 'It's none of your business.' She walked faster. 'Or mine, if you must know. The past is past.'

'You know about it.'

'I don't listen to gossip. But you're barking up the wrong tree here, mister.' Her Cornish accent had come back in her fury. 'Let things lie. Go and paint what you bloody like, but leave things lie. And don't ever talk to me again. Not ever.'
They were at the door. She stopped, and looked up at him, like an angry dog ready to bite. He suddenly saw her father in her.

'Mind your own bloody business,' he heard her swear as she burst through the door of the bank.

17

'I don't listen to gossip …'

Simon replayed the words on and off all the way home. There has to be gossip not to listen to. You can't help hearing what you aren't listening to. Even if it's through a wall or beside a doorway or coming up through the floorboards when you're in bed.

'She picked up the baby …' Put your hands over your ears. 'Went out across the moor …' Hum a loud tune. 'Went to the mine shaft.' Stick your fingers in until they hurt. 'Took the baby out of the bundle …' Pull the pillow over your head. 'And dropped him down into the darkness …' Noooooooooooo. That's the thing you don't want to hear, you want to unhear. The gossip you never heard, and can't forget. There for ever. So she knew. But that was all he had gained. It wasn't her, Simon was sure of it.

Grace was waiting for him when he arrived back at the flat.

'Can't give you any more money. Your mother would boil me in oil.'

'I didn't come for money.'

'What then?'

'A cup of tea, maybe?'

She sat on the sofa with her thin legs tucked up underneath her.

'I think Jo's pregnant.'

Simon's eyes closed in pain. Grace had no sense of inhibition or mercy.

'Why?'

'Oh, I saw her the other night, puking up in the harbour. And she was with some right old scum.'

Simon's eyes opened again in surprise.

'Oh, nothing permanent I shouldn't think. Just passing the time. So, is she?'

'Why don't you ask her?'

'God, she is then. That's why you dumped her. You're even more of a bastard than I thought.'

There was no sting in the words, just the usual cool assessment. Grace took a sip of tea and looked up maliciously.

'Mum'll fucking kill you.'

'Why?'

'If someone else has your babies. She always thought she would.'

'No she didn't.'

'That's what she told me once.'

'That's rubbish,' said Simon hotly, 'you don't know what you're talking about. Jane never wanted anyone's babies.'

There was a pause. Grace took another sip of tea.

'Christ. I'm sorry Grace. I didn't mean it like that.'

'No offence. You're probably right. She always said I was a mistake. "Too much rum one night darling". I heard her saying to some prick at a party, "She was my Bacardi baby".'

Simon jumped up. 'Come on, let's go for a walk.'

'I hate walks.'

'Just for once. Let's get all this crap out of our heads.'

Grace looked up in surprise. 'OK.'

They strode across the long sandy beach and up onto the headland beyond. The wind was strong but mild. Grace as usual was wearing the bare minimum, but she didn't seem cold. They sat down on a granite ledge to look back over the beach towards the town.

'What shall I do Grace?'

She leant down and picked a piece of grass, then started tying it in knots. 'Not my problem really,' she said at last. They watched the slow rollers coming into the sand, and the scatter of surfers waiting there to harvest them. Grace carried on: 'But you must stop being a bastard to Jo. She seems nice. She needs to know where she is. Do you love her?'

Simon gazed ahead. He and Grace had never talked like this. It was easy outside where they didn't have to meet each other's eyes.

'I honestly don't know.'

'You'd know if you did. I feel sorry for her.'

'Why?'

'You aren't exactly easy to love. It's hard to know who you are. I've known you all my life and I don't know you at all. You're like soap in the shower.'

'Thanks. At least I'm clean. And useful. That's the nicest thing you've ever said about me.'

Grace looked at him closely to be sure he was joking.

'Come on, let's go back. I can't get my head round being your agony aunt.'

'Thanks. I mean it.'

'Ring her up. As soon as you get back. Don't put it off. No excuses.'

'OK, OK.'

She gave a little smile.

As soon as he got back to the flat Simon took out his maps again and laid them on the table. There had been another place. Not Menwartha. Not Winnard where the straight old farming family still defied the elements and milked cows. Another one. He took out his compass again. There. Bosmergy.

He idly opened the post he had thrown onto the table that morning. There was a letter from the head teacher of Simon's school, and he thought it would be about Grace, as it had often been before. Then he checked himself. The hangover of life with

Jane never seemed to fade. Grace was officially no longer his problem or even his business as far as school was concerned.

Dear Simon,

I'm sorry to say that due to budget restrictions we have had to look closely at every department with a view to possible economies …

Great. That ratcheted up the stakes at the Dangerfield even further. There would be no more financial safety-net after the summer term. He ought to be working, not wasting his time chasing shadows and upsetting innocent people. He should at least put it aside until the whole exhibition was packed up and ready to go. So …

Bosmergy, then. Two daughters, and a son who would never come back to the Cornish hills. It looked very close to Jo's cottage on the map, though he could not place it in his memory. He could not settle. Grace's voice resounded in his head.

Five minutes later he rang the gallery. He greeted Jo cheerfully. She thought he sounded pleased with himself, which made her reach for something spiteful to say.

'Your paintings are getting rid of our customers in record time,' she said.

'What d'you mean?'

Briefly Jo described the reaction of her recent visitor. Simon was so quiet that she thought for a moment she had been cut off.

'Simon?'

'Did she have the newspaper with her?'

'Yes. Why?'

'How old? Roughly?'

His vehemence took her by surprise, but she responded without hesitation.

'Middle-aged. You wouldn't have noticed her. She might have

served you in Tesco yesterday – she's the sort of woman men just don't see. Why?'

'Tell me about it again.'

She sighed but did so in more detail.

'Christ.'

'What? What Simon?'

'That was *her*. I'd bet anything.'

'Who?'

'Which way did she go?'

'I didn't look. What are you on about? Who was she?'

'Did she look really upset?'

'I told you she did.'

'Christ ...'

'Simon ...'

'I will tell you, Jo, but I can't yet. I can't.'

'Fine. OK.'

'Thanks. Jo?'

'What?'

'I'm sorry. I'm sorry I've been such a shit. I'll talk to you soon. It's nearly over. Promise. I'll tell you all about it. I really will.'

She caught her breath before answering, but he had gone.

18

Ten minutes later he parked like a thief where Jo would not see his car if she came home, and carefully skirted her cottage. Bosmergy was just off the lane leading higher up the hill, where even the lush undergrowth gave out and nothing more than heather and bracken and scrubby gorse grew wild. A side turning between high hedges led to the farmhouse.

It was detached, a long stone building with small sash windows which were old and peeling, giving it a blind appearance. The farm cottage he had seen marked on the old map was across the lane, roofless now and filled with weeds. The washing line was heavy with clothes of various sizes. A broken down car sat in the long grass, and the rusty carcase of a motorbike peeped out from a patch of nettles. The garden was overgrown and full of toys, and a shiny new swing dangled in the side lawn. A radio was blaring from inside, and the sound swelled as the front door opened and a woman came out, cradling a small child. She stood on the front path and looked at Simon without expression. She wore loose knitted clothes in a variety of colours and her hair was in dreadlocks tied up with broad purple ribbon. Her eyes were bright blue.

'Hello,' he said. She did not reply. 'I was just having a look at the old place.'
'Why?'

He sought for an excuse.

'My family used to live here.'

'Richards's' she said with a local accent. Simon cursed inwardly. He hadn't counted on local knowledge. 'Who are you then?' she went on. 'You don't look like any Richards I know. Jonathan's been dead for years. There's no other men your age. Don't I know your face?'

'I don't think so. They were very distant relatives. I don't live around here,' Simon floundered on.

'Yeah? You look like someone I know. Don't mind if I don't ask you in, by the way, but it's a bit of a mess inside.'

'No, not at all. Have you had the farmhouse long?'

'About five years I think. Seems longer. It isn't mine, of course. Even I wouldn't leave it in a state like this.'

'Whose is it?'

'His Lordship's. Why do you ask? You should know that if you're family.'

Simon hadn't been prepared for such bright and keen intelligence. He started thinking anxiously how to get away. She readjusted the child and looked more closely at him, 'You're no Richards. You haven't got the face. What are you? DSS?'

'Christ no.'

'No, you don't look like one of them either. So what do you really want?'

Her eyes would not be diverted, and he felt suddenly small and exposed.

'I'm looking for …'

She waited while he threw various plausible stories around his mind, finding that none of them would fit. She kept her gaze on him with a half-smile, as if she knew what was happening.

' … ghosts.' he said at last, with no idea that he was going to say it.

Her smile broadened. 'Ghosts eh? You won't find many of them up here. They'd have to be tough little buggers to spend more than a few winters up at Bosmergy. The damp and the wind would get to them too in the end.' She paused and put the child down on the grass. He crawled towards a plastic hammer and started beating it on a rock, singing in time with the blows.

She looked back at Simon. 'I think you're out of luck. I'd know by know if there was anything spooky about the house. It's hard to tell sometimes because it's so old and draughty, but there's no-one here I can think of who isn't alive.' A child's voice called to her from the house. She yelled back, then looked at Simon once more in her coolly appraising way.

'I've got you now,' she said. 'You're the one who fell down the mine shaft. Aren't you?'

Simon nodded.

'Do you want a coffee? If you can stand the mess?'

'OK.'

Inside was gloomy and warm, smelling of onions and wood smoke. There was a pine table near the front window, covered in papers, childrens' drawings, and dirty plates.

'What's your name?' said the woman as she made space for him and moved a cat from the chair.

'Simon. What's yours?'

'Eve. How did you manage to fall in? I'm glad you did, mind. I didn't even know it was there. It could have been one of the kids. They sometimes disappear for hours up here and I've no idea where they go.'

'How many have you got?'

'Four,' she said, tipping coffee grounds into a glass cafetière. 'Which reminds me … Morvah!' she shouted suddenly.

'What?' answered a girl's truculent voice from upstairs.

'Keep an eye on Tregenna. He's outside on the grass. You can see him better from up there.'

'I'm reading.'

Eve didn't reply.

'It feels quite cosy,' said Simon, for something to say.

'There's no wind today for a change. You live down in town?'
Simon nodded. 'You'd never know what it was like up here. Even
the houses further down the lane don't have it like we do. Up here
there's no trees, nothing to stop the wind. It beats on the house so
hard you'd swear it had moved by morning. Takes bits of roof
sometimes. His Lordship's men are a bit slow in fixing it. There's
still a big lump of turf on the back roof from last winter. The rain
hits the wall side-on, and the damp runs down inside like a river.
Everything rattles. If it was blowing now we'd have to be shouting
at each other to be heard. And it goes on like that for weeks
sometimes.'

'Isn't that a bit frightening?'

'Yeah. More than a bit. It's like living in a bloody shipwreck.'

'Why do you stay?'

'Find me another long let I can afford with four kids and couple
of dogs. I'm on my own. There's not exactly a lot of choice.'
As she gave Simon his coffee, he remembered something.

'You said I haven't got a Richards' face. Do you see the family
then?'
She did not reply at once, but opened the wood-burning stove to
put another piece of firewood in.

'Brenda comes up sometimes.'

'Willie's daughter?'

'Yes. She only lives in town. But she never comes in. Never
talks to me. Just comes up once in while and stands there, across
the lane, just looking. The kids usually go out and make nuisances
of themselves until she goes away again.'

'How do you know who she is?'

'Roger from Winnard knows her. He comes in here occasionally
for a coffee and a chat when his wife's not looking. She thinks I'm
an evil hippy witch of course,' she added with a grin.

'Was there any particular … gossip about the Richards?' he said,
as lightly as he could. She turned the blue lamps of her eyes onto
him at once, wary again.

'Mum,' came the voice from upstairs, 'did you say Treg was on the grass?'

'Yes,' she shouted back.

'Well he's not there now.'

'Bugger,' she said getting up.

'May I use your toilet?' said Simon.

'Yeah. Upstairs, turn left.'

She went outside to look for the child.

The bathroom justified Eve's opinion, draughty and icy cold. Through the open door of the bedroom as he passed he saw the author of the voice curled up reading in a window seat. He smiled vaguely and she cast him a cool disinterested glance.

'Hello Simon,' she said. He jumped. 'How do you know my name?'

'I'm in your class for art, remember?' She went back to her book. Typical. There was no such thing as anonymity in this place. Tomorrow everyone would know where he'd been and what he wanted to know. And the day after probably they would be linking his name with Eve's. He sighed.

Eve came back in and gave the child a biscuit. She looked at Simon without warmth.

Yeah,' she said sitting down, 'there was gossip. All sorts. They weren't a happy family. But who's to judge anyone? Have you got a family?'

'Not really.'

'You haven't a clue then. It can be hard. Bloody hard.'

Simon took one more chance.

'I heard she lost a baby once. Brenda, that is.'

'Yeah,' said Eve, 'I heard that too. But if she doesn't want to talk about it I'm certainly not going to.' She pulled back her chair. 'I'm sorry but I'd better start getting tea together. The others will be back in a minute.'

Simon took his cue and got up to go.

'Thanks for the coffee.'

She gazed at him once more, for an uncomfortable length of time.
'Yeah.'

Simon drew up outside the Trencoth Retirement Home, thinking that he wasn't cut out to be a private eye. The deliberate intrusion into the privacy of strangers was almost more uncomfortable than he could bear. He had been brought up to respect such things, to keep conversations away from personal probing, and the inhibition was still strong. Even the building was intimidating, formerly a sprawling hotel ruining the looks of a granite headland, but now a manicured institution with tightly mown lawns and bright gravel drives and uniformed women striding purposefully about. He sat in the car for several minutes steeling himself to enter the bright conservatory and present himself at the desk.

In the corridor the smell was of pine freshness on a bed of gravy and green vegetables. Beneath this was the unique smell of old people, which made Simon want to shy like a colt. His mother lived in a place like this, though he hardly ever went to see her. She didn't seem to recognise him when he did go, but just stared at him with an awful intensity. When he moved to go she always tried to grab him, and if she succeeded she was hard to dislodge. Mostly she was quiet, but sometimes she shouted without warning, obscenities, blasphemy, hatred, tearful love. And then the silence again and the stubborn holding.

Her home was just like this one, corridors, clean surfaces, smiling young women, blank faces in an arc around the television. Last time he had seen his mother she had sat politely for several minutes, and then suddenly hit him in the face. A moment later she was once more smiling the bland smile she kept for visiting strangers.

'Willie Richards?' he asked the third smiling woman he had met.

It hadn't been hard to trace him. There were only a few old people's homes in the area, and he found the right one on the telephone at the third attempt. He passed an old Cornish woman with white hair plaited across her head, rambling to herself in a chair. He wondered if she was Queenie.

'I think he's out on the terrace,' smiled the woman. 'Come this way.' She was dark and pretty and Simon was happy to follow. They went through a sliding double-glazed door and found themselves on a paved patio overlooking a sunny garden. The lawn was shining with green and tame birds sang from the bushes. Here and there old people were sitting in chairs and wheelchairs. Some were talking to each other, bright and birdlike themselves. Others were soft and fleshy like melted waxworks. Yet others were slumped forward, seemingly unconscious, with the sun playing on their wispy hair.

Willie was at the other end of the terrace. He looked like a farmer from a children's storybook. He had a rosy face and apple cheeks, and was wearing an old tweed jacket over a collarless white shirt. On his head was a matching tweed hat. Hair which was still dark protruded from the sides of it.

'Willie,' said the girl loudly, 'you've got a visitor.' She looked at Simon for a prompt.

'It's Simon,' he stage-whispered to her, 'I rang yesterday.'

'It's SIMON,' she repeated. 'He's dropped in to see you.'

From its apathetic middle-distance stare, Willie's face suddenly assumed an air of kindly joviality, deep crows' feet at his eyes, apple-cheeks shining. He beamed up at Simon with signs of instant recognition.

'Oh yeh?'

'I brought you some cream.' Simon had thought hard about his choice of gift. In the end he had decide that for a countryman a small tub of yellow crusted cream would be appropriate. The nurse frowned slightly at so much cholesterol. Willie's smile did not waver.

'Oh yeh?'

Simon was suddenly afraid that that was all he could say. He opened the batting.

'I've been staying up by Bosmergy.'

Willie's eyes seemed to focus a little more, though nothing else changed.

'Oh yeh?'

'Yes, a friend of mine's got a place up there. The cottage by the moor,' Simon paused. 'You used to live at the farmhouse. You remember the cottage?'

'Oh yeh. The cottage. Yeh.'

'Did you ever live at the cottage?'

'The cottage? We never lived there.'

'No, of course, you were up at the farmhouse.'

'That's right. We lived at the farmhouse.'

Simon cast an eye at the nurse, but she was only concerned that everyone was still smiling. She was used to conversations which didn't make sense.

'With the children...'

'With the children, that's right.' He was opening up. 'You live at the cottage? Nice up there. Windy, mind.'

'I hear your daughter came to see you yesterday.'

The receptionist had given him that. And the following.

'You've got grandchildren now I hear.'

'Oh yeh.'

'A granddaughter living around here.'

'Oh yeh. Near grown now. She comes here to see me. I say, she comes here.' This was spoken as if to clinch an argument, aimed at the nurse, who started from a private reverie.

'Who's that Willie?'

'Girl. Granddaughter.'

'Oh, the one with the ... hair. Susan? Sammy? Stacey, that's it.

'Yes, I've seen her once or twice.'

Stacey? It couldn't be. His mind raced back at once to the school open evening, to the shapeless woman with the uncomfortable stare. He remembered Jo's description of the gallery visitor. It couldn't be. It had to be. He pulled his whirling thoughts together and pressed on while he had the chance. 'Were there any other grandchildren?'

The nurse, now listening, seemed suddenly aware of Simon's ignorance. She gave him a preliminary stare, unsure how to respond.

'No,' said Willie. 'Only the one. Just one.'

'No others at all?'

'No.'

'What, none?'

'Mr ... I'm sorry, I've forgotten what you said your name was ...' The nurse was becoming agitated, but Simon was too committed to stop.

'I thought there was another baby. Before Stacey ...'

Willie was still smiling the smile of an honest open-faced yeoman.

'I think Willie's a bit tired ...'

'What happened to the baby? The other one? The first one?'

'Please ...'

'What became of the other baby?'

In a horrible instant Willie's face changed shape. The friendly yeoman was gone. In its place was a completely different expression, sharp, angry, pointed and mean. His eyes had focussed and narrowed, staring hard at Simon above a mouth which was clamped into a tight line, turned down at the edges, suddenly cruel. His broad farmer's hands twisted the edges of his blanket in a grip which was still strong. His voice was dark with emotion.

'Who are you?'

19

Stacey's here Mum,' said Grace as she went into the sitting room. The television was up high and Jane was half-way through her second bottle. She glared mistily at Grace.

'So?'

'Oh, nothing.' Stacey had stayed with Grace since they were at primary school, on and off, especially when things got too bad at home. A few times Grace had returned the visits. But, of course, only when Gary was at sea. Nothing would persuade Grace there when he was at home.

They took a DVD up to Grace's room and arranged themselves comfortably to watch it. Their friendship was born of opposites. Stacey was full-bodied in contrast to Grace's brittle slimness, she was earthy while Grace lived in her own world, she was lazy while Grace was fiercely industrious. Stacey had been first into cigarettes, drink, sex and a handful of different drugs. None of these appealed to Grace. Yet their relationship was steady and unquestioned. They could talk or be quiet, laugh, scream, or share their deepest fears. They were sure in the comfort of each other's presence.

They barely spoke during the film. Grace made coffee and smuggled biscuits out of the kitchen. They could hear Jane two floors below having a row with someone on the telephone.

'I had such a weird dream last night,' said Stacey suddenly.

Grace turned to look her in the face.

'I dreamed that dream I sometimes have, you know, when my dad comes back from sea?'
Grace nodded. Stacey's parents had split before her first birthday, but her father had kept in close touch with his daughter until one winter's day when she was seven. His boat was later discovered at the bottom of the Celtic sea, though no bodies ever came home for burial.

'Gary was being his usual bastard self to Mum, and I was like watching from above?' Stacey was talking quietly into her own lap, occasionally looking to Grace for confirmation. 'Our street was all quiet except for those two going on. And then Dad sort of stepped into the light and started walking up the street really slowly. I knew he was looking for our house, but he was sort of blind and deaf, because he was a ghost. He had ... weed in his hair and everything. And I was calling him, shouting so he'd know which house to come to. But he couldn't hear me.' She stopped for a moment to remind herself. 'He'd got to the end of the path and was sort of hesitating. Gary and my mum suddenly shut up, like they knew he was there. Listening. Everybody was listening. I was just ... holding my breath. Then I woke up, of course, in this huge sweat.'
Grace smiled.

'Maybe one night he'll come right in and kick Gary's brains out,' Stacey went on.

'You can stay here as long as you want.'

'I can't leave Mum for too long. He really hurts her.'

There was a pause, and they stopped talking about parents. But later, when they were snuggled down in their sleeping bags, Stacey's mind went back to her dream.

'I used to go out with my dad on his boat sometimes.'

'What fishing?'

'No, not the big boat. He had a little punt and sometimes he'd row me just out of the harbour and a little way into the bay. We'd fish and stuff. It was nice.'

'Did you ever catch anything?' said Grace sleepily.

'No – yeah!' she said with sudden animation. 'One day when I wasn't looking he managed to fiddle this humongous great fish – a pollock or something – on to my line and pretended I'd caught it.' She laughed quietly at the memory. 'He was so great. Everybody liked him. He used to help out on the lifeboat and everything. He had a massive funeral – except he wasn't there of course.'

'Why didn't he stick with your mum?'

There was a pause. 'It sounds stupid,' said Stacey, 'he was probably too nice for her. I don't really remember. After that she always picked up on pond life, as if she thought she like – deserved it.'

'Grown-ups are so fucked up. You'd think they'd be able to see what they were doing to themselves.'

They fell silent again.

'I don't think she likes your dad's paintings.'

'Why?'

'I was there when she opened the paper the other day. She stared at it for ages then burst into tears and ran out. When I had a look it was just one of your dad's abstract things. I didn't get it at all.'

'No,' said Grace, thinking suddenly of *Painting No 5* 'No point in asking me. I've never got it.'

'She's been really interested in your dad ever since he went down that hole. She asked me loads of things about him.'

'What sort of stuff?'

'What kind of teacher he is. What he's like. Stuff like that.'

'You asleep?'

The wind twitched at the branches outside the house, and a shower began its pattern on the window.

'No. Maybe she fancies him.'

For a moment they entertained the idea, then they both began to laugh.

'Christ,' said Stacey, 'yeah, right. Imagine those two together!'

Jo turned the radio off. It was getting late. The silence was worse, and a few minutes later she turned it on again. She poured out some more wine. Guilt flooded through her with the liquid. She'd read all the books. She could picture the alcohol seeping across her placenta like a curse.

The telephone was on the table. It fascinated her, like a hole through to an alien world. She walked around and about it, not willing to see it. It hadn't rung all evening, and wasn't going to now. Once or twice she took determined steps towards it, numbers ready in her head. She had even sat down beside it, but couldn't pick it up. She put her head in her hands. I can't do this, she thought, and repeated aloud to the empty cottage, 'I can't do this.' Look at me, sorted Jo, flapping like a salmon in a net. One call and it would be beyond remedy. She made fresh coffee and sat down to sip it. Who to please? Herself? Simon? Nadia? The half-intoxicated half-life inside her? She was desperate for help, but didn't want to talk to anyone. Except one.

Her hand reached out on its own and dialled the number. It rang for a while, and she imagined it echoing through the familiar house. She had worked out what to say, how to lead around to it. It was so important to present it in the right way. If it started on a negative line, that would colour the whole thing forever. So start light, ease into it, don't make it sound like a crisis

The familiar voice answered, full of anxiety, repeating nervous 'hellos'. They grew more shrill as no answer came. Jo's mind had blanked as soon as she heard the sound. Finally the words came, 'Mum? Hello … I'm pregnant ...'
And for a while that was all she could say.
There was a mirror above the washbasin in the studio's cramped

toilet. Simon paused after washing his hands and stared at his own face. He looked hard into his own eyes for clues. Then he sat on a stool and stared in an unfocussed way at one of his own pictures.

The exhibition was ready, at the removers ready to be cased up and taken to London. The five new paintings were already returned from Ti's, boxed up ready for transit. He badly wanted to look at them again, to try to retrace the energy he had poured into them. He was tired again, as tired as he had been after the fall. After the fall.

He would have liked to imagine that fate had chosen him, except that he didn't believe in fate. Or that God had led him to the place where his moral strength would be put to the test, but he had no faith in God either. Or even that the ivory dome in the mud had called out to him from below to lay its ghost to rest. If only he could believe in ghosts. But he couldn't.

Once long ago someone had asked him what he felt 'in his heart of hearts', and Jane had laughed and immediately responded that Simon did not have a heart of hearts. He remembered being somehow pleased at the time. No-one could ever penetrate the crevasses in that blue sheet of ice.

Except Jane herself of course. She knew all the secret ways. For her he would sweat, cry, rage, plead, or throw back his head and shout. Even that evening they had had a yelling match on the phone about some forgotten bill, nothing special. It had never been less than intense. For her all his emotions had been exposed, dragged out by their bleeding roots and stuffed back in any old how. For her all his self-regard and dignity, petulance and conceit had long ago had its come-uppance. The drama, the ecstasy, the despair, the rawness and intensity were scenes from another more passionate life, acted out by a different cast. That Simon was no more, behind him. Gone.

That was what Jo could not understand, and he could not explain. Only once in your life could you let those wild horses out of their stall. After that they were over the horizon and gone. Jo, even Jo's baby, his baby, were folded in plastic, they could slip easily in and out of his life without any sharp edges to snag on. He himself was worn smooth, emotionally cool, morally neutral. He could cope with anything. Anything except, perhaps, for a helpless curve of a small fleshless hand.

And what help had he given to the call in the dark? He had helped himself instead, happy for it to trigger a new era of artistic creativity, thrilled with his own sensitivity. His passion had been sufficient in itself. His brief career as a detective had ended soon enough too, an ignominious retreat from a twilight home, running stupidly for the car even though no-one was chasing him. So what.

He had other itches to scratch. His ego was hungry and beginning to sniff a feast. London covered many worse consciences than his in its folds. It was time to leave Cornwall's fantasy world behind and sharpen up. He hadn't asked to be an artist, but he was. He would do what artists do, and others could clean up after him. Meanwhile it was his last chance to tinker with the angular blue painting still on the easel before it was packed away. He had just begun to mix colours when the sudden ring of the bell made him jump and swear.

20

He opened the door to find two strangers on the pavement, silhouetted by the street light in the wet mist. A sparely-built man was about to press the bell again. Behind him a larger woman seemed to be hanging back, although they were definitely together. A few yards up the road Simon noticed an old pickup.

'Can I help you?'

'Yeh?' The man had a London accent. 'Can we come in a minute? My partner wanted a word.'

School? Simon didn't recognise the voice. The man waited quietly, standing still.

'I am a bit busy. Will it take long?'

'Just a couple of minutes.'

'OK.'

He stood aside as the man went lightly up the stairs. The woman followed silently, and Simon realised as she passed that he knew her, but couldn't remember why or how. They stood in the middle of the studio, away from all the paintings. He looked at the couple under the light and sighed.

'Mrs Jackson ... sorry I didn't recognise you in the dark. I suppose it's about Stacey?'

She did not answer. Willie Richards' daughter. Here at last. He could see a little of her father's face in her now, although she had none of his ruthlessness. Was it about his visit? Anxiety flowed through his veins, increasing the longer Brenda Jackson stared at him without speaking. Someone had to say something.

'What's the problem?'

Gary glided out from behind her. He was in his late forties but carried no fat. His face had a slight violet tinge from a lifetime's drinking, but it was impossible to tell if he was drunk or not. Although shorter than Simon he seemed to dominate the studio. He spoke quietly, with a reasonable tone.

'You've been taking the piss,' he stated, as an agreed fact.

'No ...' said Simon. Gary came closer to him, inside the normal bounds of personal space. Simon could smell the drink on his breath. Gary looked up.

I didn't ask for your opinion,' he said patiently. As he did, his head seemed to blur. Numbness hit Simon, followed by shock and pain. He put his hand to his mouth, then saw the blood on it. Gary stood quietly, poised, Brenda Jackson a statue behind him.

'You've upset Brenda. She wants to know what you're after.' His eyes were slate-blue in a weather-beaten face.

'I'm calling the police if you're not out of here in one minute,' said Simon shakily.

'What were those pictures all about? Why were you upsetting an old man? She thinks you're having a laugh.'

'Get out of my studio. Now!' said Simon firmly, ending in a cough of pain as Gary's small hard fist drove deep into his stomach. For few moments he could only gasp, tears of pain in his eyes.

'She just wants a simple answer,' Gary went on, then winked at Simon confidentially. 'What are you up to? Eh?'

'Nothing,' said Simon when he could.

'You're not helping,' said Gary. 'What happened when you went down the shaft? What did you see down there?'
Simon hesitated. 'Don't make me hit you again, my friend,' said Gary. 'Don't forget, I know already.'

Simon closed his eyes against the pain. 'I didn't mean to find it,' he mumbled. 'I didn't know whose it was, or what it was doing down there. I was just trying to find out. I didn't know it was hers. If it was.' Gary continued to stare at him from a few inches' distance. 'I tried to forget about it, but I couldn't. I didn't mean to upset anyone.' Simon's strength was starting to return.

'But you have,' said Gary, 'haven't you.'

'I'm sorry then,' said Simon. 'I won't tell anybody. Nobody will know. Now will you please get out of my studio.'

Gary did not seem to have heard him. He took his hypnotic gaze away from Simon and walked around the studio with his back to him. He was wearing a denim jacket, black T-shirt, jeans, and trainers, and made almost no sound as he went. His body was simian, as if he could climb up the walls of the studio as easily as he walked on the floor. He stopped in front of the painting on the easel.

'What's that worth?' he said without turning round.

'I don't know. Two or three grand. Why?'

'Dear, oh dear,' said Gary, 'two or three grand for that? Christ. I can fish for a month in winter, all weathers, and not make two or three grand. That's disgusting.'

'It's what I do,' said Simon. 'Each to his own … don't do that!' Gary had moved so quickly that his foot was back on the floor by the time the easel was falling, and the painting – its ragged hole like a wound – was still spinning to the floor.

'Now what's it worth?'

'You've gone too far now. That's criminal damage. I'm calling the police.'

Gary walked unhurriedly up to him as he picked up the telephone. He stood relaxed before him, and even in the moment Simon could not help admiring his animal efficiency. He knew Gary could kill him if he wanted to, quickly, quietly, without even breaking sweat. Having no choice he started to punch in the numbers. Gary let him go to the last nine before waving his right hand in the air as a half-comic distraction and driving his bony forehead once more into Simon's unprotected face.

The lights swam, and blood ran down into his mouth. He picked up a paint rag and held it blindly in front of his face to stem the flow. Blood dripped onto the bare wood floor. Gary calmly checked that the call had not connected, then put the receiver down. Through his muffled mouth Simon said, 'Either you'll have to kill me or I'm getting the police onto you for assault. You'd better get out of here now.'

But Gary was not listening. He was talking rapidly to Brenda, who hadn't yet said a word or shown any emotion. He turned back to Simon.

'You'll need a coat. And some boots, if you've got any.'

'I'm not going anywhere,' said Simon, 'you are.'

'I'll count to ten,' said Gary, in a bored tone.

'I'm not going anywhere,' said Simon again. 'You can't make me.'

Gary looked up, relishing the challenge for a moment. But he was in a hurry. 'I'm a very patient man,' he explained, 'but you're starting to annoy me. If you aren't out of the door and in my pickup in ten seconds, I'll do the rest of your paintings, and then I'll start on you. Did you get all that?'

'What do you want with me?'

'You'll see.'

'Mrs Jackson,' he appealed.

'... five ... six ... seven ...,' said Gary, 'eight'. Their eyes met. 'If you come now it'll be all over in an hour. You can come back and paint what the fuck you like. If you don't, it won't just be the pictures, or you,' he said very quietly. 'It'll be that stuck-up kid of yours as well. She's been asking for a good slap for years. I know where she is. Don't think I wouldn't do it.'

'What do you want?'

'You'll see. Come on.'

He eyed the crates of finished paintings.

After a moment Simon's eyes dropped. He turned to pick his old jacket off its hook.

'Where are we going?'

He sat in the middle seat of the pick-up. The streets were dark and quiet and the windscreen wipers were the only sound. Next to him Brenda sat staring impassively into the rain. Gary drove fast in the direction of the harbour, then turned down a track into a yard behind the quay. There was the usual assortment of sheds, nets, trailers, and broken-down pieces of machinery. He pulled up outside a garage and got out. Simon made to slide out after him.

'Where are you off?'

'Isn't this where we're going?' said Simon.

'No. Get back in and sit quiet.'

Simon and Brenda sat without looking at each other, Simon still rubbing his bruises and dabbing at the blood. Soon they could hear Gary furiously throwing bits of timber, tools and other things into the back. He got back in.

'You got everything else?' he said to Brenda. She indicated a carrier bag by her feet. 'Right.'

They drove off. After a few minutes Gary, whose temper seemed to be still rising, said, 'Well?'

'What?'

'Aren't you going to apologise?'

'Who to?' said Simon, the act of speech paining him. 'What for?'

'To her!' shouted Gary. 'Tell her why you've been winding her up with your pictures and all that.'

'How? What am I supposed to have done?' said Simon.

'Don't make me madder, you little cunt. Why did you have to drag it all up again?'

'I didn't know it was hers. I didn't know whose it was. All I was trying to do was find out.'

'Why couldn't you mind your own fucking business? Why couldn't you just forget it?'

'I just couldn't,' mumbled Simon. 'I spent hours down there with its body. I thought I was going to die too. How could I just forget it?'

'Him,' said Brenda.

'Do you know what you've put her through? Have you any idea?'

There was a long pause before Simon said no.

'She's been through hell because of you. Bloody hell.' Gary was driving fast though the outskirts.

'I didn't mean to fall down there. I haven't said a word to anyone.'

'You'd better not have.'

Simon turned to Brenda. 'I am really am sorry. Not because of him. Sorry about your little boy.'

Brenda stared ahead, but harshly wiped away a tear with the back of her hand.

Gary roared. 'Don't start her crying again! That's all I need. Shit! Shut up you stupid cow, shut up or I'll stop the truck and hit you. I will …' He slammed on the brakes. Brenda held up her hand before he could stop.

'I'm alright.'

He speeded up again. The road led out of town in a familiar direction, and suddenly Simon felt more fear than he had ever known. His legs went to water and he felt sick. He tried to keep the tremble out of his voice as he said:

'Why are we going up here?'

'Unfinished business,' said Gary brutally.

The room was dark. Grace woke to the sound of crying.

'Don't. Stop it.'

'Look, pissoff!'

'Mum, Mum!'

She got out of bed and padded silently across to where Stacey lay on the spare bed in her sleeping bag. She was quiet for a moment, but suddenly turned over again and cried out. Her long hair was moist with sweat. Grace went to the bathroom and wet a flannel in cold water, which she carefully squeezed out. She knelt by Stacey's head, cooling her forehead. 'It's all right. Don't worry. It's alright.'

Stacey calmed almost at once.

'Mum?'

'It's all right.'

'Has he gone?'

'He's gone now,' Grace reassured her, as she had done often before. Stacey's breathing slowed down. Grace stroked her hair gently for a few moments, then tiptoed back to bed.

21

The pick-up bumped up the lane across the moors and stopped close to the shaft. Gary killed the lights at once. It had stopped raining but it was still cloudy and dark. For a moment they all sat like stones. Simon was the first to speak, and he turned again to Brenda.

'Tell me what happened.'

Brenda opened her mouth, then shut it in a tight line of self-control.

'I have to know.'

'I'll tell him,' said Gary, 'not that it's any of his business. And not a sound out of you, all right, otherwise you can forget the whole thing.' Gary told Simon the bare facts while Brenda listened without a sound. Gary only knew the story as he understood it, from the man's angle. Silently she let her memory fill in the spaces.

Gary knew that she had slept with one of the contract men who came to cut the silage at Bosmergy, and assumed that he had taken her unwillingly, as he himself might have done. But it hadn't been like that. The contract man had been different, full of laughter, glad-faced and young. She had led him on, amazed to feel loving arms around her body for the first time, excited and terrified of discovery. She cornered him at every opportunity, and he laughed and submitted, calling her a nymphomaniac. At the end of the week he had gone on to another farm, and no-one had found out. She knew he would never come back, and didn't want him to, not to a world where no-one ever laughed.

Gary said that her pregnancy was a surprise, and that it didn't show because she was naturally stout. But she knew she was pregnant before his shiny tractor left the yard for the last time. She remembered how delicious it had felt when the movements in her stomach began, and gradually turned over the weeks into strong motions, the way she had seen a cow's sides bulge as a calf moved inside her. She held her arms over her stomach closely and hard when her father hit her. She had something of her own, at last, to protect.

Gary merely said she gave birth at home. He didn't know how hard she had held on until her father was out milking with Jonathan helping, and how Rosemary had come home unexpectedly and found her howling on the bathroom floor. Rosemary had locked the door from the inside, and later when her father tried to break in pulled a cabinet across it. It seemed to go on forever, the tearing pain, the beating on the door panels, her father's roaring voice in her ears. When the child was born at last, Rosemary yelled at him that it was a boy. The house fell quiet. When they ventured out together with the baby, he was sitting in his chair. They thought he was asleep, but his eyes were open, looking straight ahead. He didn't even glance at the child.

The baby was hot and fretful. He wouldn't feed or sleep. Rosemary wanted to go for the doctor, but her father threatened her with his stick. When she tried to ring for help, he tore out the phone wires. When she offered to run for the police, Brenda stopped her. She knew she would be the one to suffer. His thin cry grew weaker. His skin was burning to the touch. After two sleepless nights, Brenda watched through a mist of exhaustion, almost too tired to care, as the child slipped away.

'No-one is to know,' said her father, waking her with a blow. 'No-one.' He told her to pick up the child and follow him. She wrapped him up carefully against the chilly mist. In the dead of night they stumbled across the moor to the place her father knew. He took the bundle from her and dropped it into the earth. Nothing more was said. Rosemary left home the same day, never to return. Jonathan joined the army. Brenda was left behind, destined to fulfil her dead mother's role and help on the farm and in the house. She continued to look after her father as before. They never spoke of the baby. They hardly spoke at all.

One morning a man came up the lane in a van, selling fish, while her father was milking. A week later Brenda packed a bag while her father was in town, and walked all the way to the fisherman's house. She never went near Bosmergy again. Her father passed her in the street without another word, and made no response even when she sent him a card to tell him of Stacey's birth. When he was finally taken into the nursing home she dutifully visited him every week, though they mostly sat in silence. Stacey knew nothing of the baby and had recently insisted on seeing her grandfather too, taking a perverse pleasure in the distress it caused Brenda. Rosemary would not answer letters. Jonathan died. Life went on.

'Nice chap,' concluded Gary. Simon thought again of his ruddy face and his apple-cheeked smile, the jolly storybook farmer.

'And the toy?' said Simon. Gary was at a loss, but Brenda's voice was under control.

'I bought it in town and dropped it down after.'

Simon though hard before asking the next question, but asked it anyway. 'Did the baby die of … would it have died anyway?'
But Brenda's lips were pursed once more in a tight white line.

'Never mind,' said Gary. 'Brenda's had the fear of God from that day to this that someone would find out, and put her in prison. Even if it wasn't her fault. Which it wasn't,' he added angrily.

'Wouldn't it have been better to tell someone and put an end to it?'

'Who'd believe her?' Suddenly Gary opened the driver's door. 'Come on,' he said, 'I sail at three.'

'Why are we here?' asked Simon, fear returning.

'She wants him put to rest properly. She wants him properly buried, so no-one will ever find him again. Since you've been down there already, and caused all this trouble, we thought you'd be just the man for the job. Are you sure you haven't told anyone else? Not your girlfriend or anyone?'

'No,' said Simon, instantly regretting it, 'nobody knows.'

Gary looked at him closely for a moment, then shouted at Brenda.

'Come on, get out, we haven't got all night. Here ...' he said, handing them both torches from the cab. Brenda got out slowly, zombie-like, staring ahead, with the carrier bag. They went in line towards the wire fence and stopped. The night had calmed down.

'OK,' said Brenda, rummaging in her bag.

'What are we doing?' said Simon.

'We're doing the job properly,' said Gary.

'Christ ...' Simon gasped, as Brenda took a small crucifix out of her bag and set it up on a stone. She set two large candles on either side of the crucifix, rubbing them on the rock so that they were flat on the bottom and stayed upright.

'We can't do this,' said Simon.

'Why not?'

'We haven't got a vicar,' he answered stupidly.

'Never mind,' said Gary, 'we'll have to pretend we're at sea.' He was glaring at Simon in the dark, not in fury but in sudden male complicity. 'Won't we?' Don't let me down, his eyes were saying. Back me up. Brenda succeeded in lighting the candles. Gary snapped out 'Let us pray.' and they lowered their heads immediately out of habit. 'Our father ... ' he began. They stumbled through the Lord's Prayer. Simon looked up at the other two to be sure he wasn't in a nightmare. Brenda's eyes were tightly shut. Gary was staring at the ground. The prayer finished.

'The Lord's my shepherd … ' Brenda struck up the psalm in a thin emotional voice. Simon followed from childhood memory. As they sang 'Yea though I walk in death's dark vale …' he saw Gary steal a look at Brenda, naked for a moment. He realised with a shock how much, in his own way, he loved her.

When the psalm was over Gary made a hesitant address, 'Lord, we commend to you the body of this innocent child … Christopher James.' Brenda sobbed at the name, but did not break down. 'Take him up … and find a place for him in Heaven. We come to put his body to rest at last in your arms … and leave his spirit in your eternal care.'

'Amen,' said Brenda. The candles flickered in the breeze. The three of them stood bowed like the hawthorn trees in the hedgerows, bent over by the endless winds.

'Phew,' said Gary in his normal voice. 'Thank fuck that's over. Get back in the cab, Brenda.'

A few minutes later Gary was a whirl of activity. Holding the torch in his left hand, he cut the strands of the barbed wire and went to the head of the shaft. He bent down to drag aside the weighted-down sheets of plywood which had been laid over the hole. Simon stood wondering whether to run for the cottage. It would only take a few moments, he could take Jo's car and drive like hell to the nearest police station, and get these crazy, crazy people locked up. But what would Gary do to Jo? Or Grace? As he hesitated Gary was suddenly beside him.

'Give me a bloody hand. Let's get this over with,' he said. Then he looked at Simon again, with his animal senses awake. 'Thinking of running off, were you? It wouldn't be clever.' Simon was still thinking of it. Suddenly Gary smiled, showing good teeth, and said in his conspiratorial way, 'Come on. It won't take a minute.'

With a sigh Simon followed him towards the edge of the mine. Halfway there he stopped dead.

'What?' said Gary.

'I can't do it,' said Simon, rigid. 'I can't go back down there. You do it.'

Gary didn't answer. Simon heard him fumbling among his clothes, then jumped as the sharp point of a knife pressed into the back of his ribcage, just hard enough to break the skin.

'Course you can.'

He pressed a little harder, and Simon's legs took him forward towards the black opening, still partly covered with boarding. He stopped again on the edge.

'Hang on.'

Gary went back to the pick-up and fetched a crowbar and a sledgehammer. He quickly beat the crowbar into the earth with great force, deep into the ground. He went back and returned with a rope and a short-handled shovel. A makeshift harness was attached to the rope, and he attached it gently to Simon's stiff body. Then he wound the rope twice around the shaft of the half-buried crowbar. It all took just a few moments. Simon was still hoping to wake from his dream when Gary handed him the shovel.

'OK?' said Gary.

'What am I supposed to do?'

'Dig a hole down there and bury him properly. So that if some other twat falls down they won't see anything. Go on, we've said our prayers, now we've got to put him to rest. When you've done, give three tugs on the rope and I'll haul you up, and then you can fuck off home.'

Simon gazed at him, trying to read his eyes. But it was dark.

'Come on,' Gary shouted in his face. 'I don't want to put another hole in your shirt.'

A sudden sweat soaked Simon's face and hands. Gary's eyes were unfathomable.

'Come on!'

Suddenly Simon moved.

'Hold that rope tight,' he said. 'I'll shout when I get to the water.' Then he turned with his back to the hole, and started to ease his legs into it. He descended slowly, holding the torch and the shovel in one hand, and fending off the rubble walls with the other. It took a long time to reach the chamber where the walls fell away.

The rain had swelled the pool, but the cavern was bigger than Simon remembered it. There was a fresh fall of orange clay on one side. He shouted, and the rope held him suspended over the pool, as his rescuer had once been. For a moment he could not orient himself. Everything looked different in the sharp light of the torch. He pushed and kicked until he made a landfall on the appropriate bank.

'Slack off.' His voice echoed up the shaft.

He did not try to lift the remains of Christopher James, but dug a mound over him, topped with some small stones he found amongst the clay. He was sweating from effort now, not fear, sticking at the task to keep thoughts away, not wishing even to look around. He patted down the top of the mound with the shovel, and said another quiet word of prayer. Only when he had finished did he suddenly think of Jo, and another small life which would never prosper.

'OK," he shouted.

He heard Gary's distorted voice, 'Have you done it properly?'

'Yes.'

'He's done it Brenda,' he heard Gary shout in the distance. 'OK. Pull on the rope … three … times.'

Even distorted by the shaft, Simon could hear a new note in Gary's voice. His mind blurred from sorrow to fright. He pulled, and then again. He felt no surprise, no shock or even numbness when, at the third pull, the rope came hissing down into the water. He felt nothing as he heard the boards being dragged over the shaft again, or when Brenda's first hysterical cries mingled with Gary's harsh response. He heard the rumble as the heavy weights were rolled back onto the boards, and soon after that the distant muffled sound of the truck. Then, for the first time since he had opened the door of his studio, it was quiet. He exhaled a long, trembling sigh.

22

From her bed Jo heard the truck in the far distance. She thought for a moment that it might be Simon, coming back at last to tell her his secrets. But no-one arrived, and after a while she was not sure she had really heard it.

It was her first night as a properly post-denial pregnant person. She had made preparations in her practical way, wine, rescue remedy, soothing music, in case it was a difficult night. But she had cried very little, and the greatest struggle was with her feelings of elation. It was like holding on to the juiciest piece of gossip ever, constantly dying to ring someone up to tell them. Above all she felt ridiculously happy. She curled up with her arms over her breasts and went to sleep smiling.

In the cab, Brenda was screaming.

'You can't do that, you can't you can't! They'll look for him. They're probably looking right now.'

'They won't look down there, will they? They pulled him out of there once. That's the last place they'd look.'

'He'll die!'

'So what? There's enough artists around, fuck knows. No-one'll miss him. And nobody will ever know.'

Brenda broke down.

'I wanted it over. I wanted it over. I've waited so long.'

'It is over. But it won't be if he goes around painting his pictures and dropping hints all over the place. He's not the sort to keep his mouth shut. You'll never sleep while he's still around. Think about it you silly cow.'

'But you've killed him … '

'No I haven't. Nobody's killed him. He's alive isn't he? If he dies, it'll be from natural causes. And suppose they ever find him down there, what'll they see? A man with a rope and harness and a shovel and a torch. They'll think he went caving or something. I've given it a bit of thought you know.'

'I never thought you'd do that. I wouldn't have come … '

'I did it for you, don't you realise? For you.'

But Brenda could not take her face out of her hands or stop sobbing. After a moment Gary said, 'Alright, look, if you want to call someone up tomorrow or better still the day after to let the little prick out, it's up to you. But make sure nobody knows you done it. I think he's learnt his lesson. But wait until I'm well out to sea. I won't be back for a bit.'

A pause fell. Brenda's sobs slowed down and stopped. She said 'Are you coming back to my place?'

'No,' said Gary, 'I'll drop you off. I've got stuff to do before I go.'

In the small terraced house Brenda wandered in a daze. She boiled a kettle and let it cool again. She opened the door to Stacey's room to hear her breathing. But Stacey wasn't there. She went downstairs, weeping freely. She sat on the sofa for an hour, but the crying would not stop. She succeeded in making a cup of tea, and let that go cold too. She noticed the time only once, to be sure Gary's boat really had gone. Then, exhausted, she took off her shoes and stretched herself wearily out on the sofa. She picked up the cold tea and took a sip, to wet her throat. It was difficult taking the cap off the small bottle, but she managed it in the end. She poured out the contents onto her chest and put them into her mouth three or four at a time, washed down with the tea. It took a while, but at last they were all gone.

Later, as the dark weariness settled over her, she remembered she had not left a note. She thought about Stacey, and Christopher James, and her own mother, and cried a little more. But her body was too far bedded down into the comforting sofa to think of raising it. She was too light to take up its burden again. Then she slipped out of mind, letting go gratefully as her body sank through layers of warmth and darkness, with a sound like organ chords played on the deepest notes. Stacey found her when she wandered in the next afternoon. Brenda was barely alive, but had no will to respond to the desperate measures of intensive care. She died that evening without recovering consciousness, Stacey, white and distraught by her side.

Jane was not pleased when Grace brought Stacey home under sedation, but she had to agree there was nowhere else for her to go. She could hardly stay at her own house, and she had abruptly refused to contemplate any contact with her aunt. Jane rang Simon for assistance, but he wasn't answering his calls. Grace took charge, dealing with the police and the hospital, the coroner and the undertaker. Gary's boat was contacted, but the police found that it had gone straight to Ireland. Gary had stepped ashore to buy cigarettes, and hadn't come back. The boat sailed on to the fishing grounds without him. The Irish police promised to keep a look out.

The next morning was fine and fresh. Jane was about to leave the two girls asleep to go to a yoga class, when there was a knock on the door and Howard walked in. He looked flushed and Jane thought he was drunk, which he was, though mostly from the night before.

'Can I come in for a minute?'

'You have,' said Jane discouragingly. Howard took no notice.

'Any chance of some coffee?' he said.

Jane pushed the coffee pot, which was still half-full, towards him.

'Simon isn't here is he?'

Jane was startled. 'Christ no. Why should he be here?'

'No, of course. I can't seem to track him down. Could you do me an enormous favour?'

The pleading in his voice made Jane look at him more closely. She forgot about yoga.

'Go on,' she said, sitting back in her chair. The curtains blew gently at the open window. Eventually Howard gathered himself and spoke, looking down at his coffee cup.

'You know what I'm like. Amongst my other blinding virtues, I'm a bloody great coward. My test results came this morning.'

'Test results?'

'I keep forgetting you and Simon don't talk. Lump-in-the-bollocks sort of test. Am I about to say goodbye to them? Are they about to say goodbye to me? That sort of thing.'

'And?' she said, less harshly.

'Oh, and while I was about it, the quack persuaded me to have a HIV test. The full monty. You see why I'm such a mess.'

'What did it say, Howard?'

'That's just it,' said Howard, with a ghastly smile, 'I haven't quite plucked up the courage to open it yet.' He reached inside the pocket of his linen jacket and pulled out an envelope. 'I know it's awfully wet of me,' he said, 'but I haven't got anybody at the moment. I didn't want to be on my absolute own when I read it. Sorry.'

Jane could cope with broken-winged birds, as long as they didn't require long term care. She reached her hand across the table and held his. He gripped it lightly, still staring downwards.

'OK,' she said. 'Do you want me to open it for you?' He nodded.

'And read it?'

'Yes. Please. Sorry.'

'Let's get it over then.'

She quickly slit the envelope with a knife and unfolded the letter. She scanned the table of figures, turned to the second page, then turned back and looked at both pages again carefully. The sound of the children playing in the next door garden drifted in through the window.

'You're clear, Howard. It's benign.'

'And the HIV?'

'Clear again. You lucky old bugger. Live to fight another day'

A huge sobbing sigh broke from Howard, and then another. He met Jane's eyes for the first time, his own swimming.

'Christ, Jane. Thanks. Thanks.'

He stood up slowly, and Jane got up to hug him. He hugged her back with his soft body.

'I'm really alright?'

'You're a fit man. If you looked after yourself you'd be A1. Knock of the booze a bit. Look who's talking. Mind you, there are occasions ...'

She went to the fridge and brought out an opened bottle of white wine, then poured out a couple of glasses.

'Here's to a life of health and self-denial,' she said.

'Amen,' said Howard, his breathing still recovering. They toasted each other and laughed, then sat down still laughing.

'Glad someone's so happy,' said Grace who had entered silently on bare feet. Her face a mask, she took some mineral water from the cupboard and went back upstairs.

'Teenage angst?' said Howard.

'No. No, worse than that. Her best friend's mother took an overdose yesterday.'

'Oh dear. Did she recover?'

Jane shook her head. 'The daughter's upstairs at the moment while they sort out what's to become of her.'

'No family?'

'No-one who's any use. Father's dead. Abusive step-father who's done a runner. Gaga grandad in a home. Aunt up the line somewhere she won't speak to. Nobody here.'

'Poor mite,' said Howard. 'Can I look at my letter now?'

He read the letter slowly twice, sipping at his wine, smiling to himself. Jane's cat wound itself around his legs.

23

Grace called in to see Jo, but found Ti sitting at the desk.

'Oh hi,' she said, 'is Jo here?'

Ti never hurried, so she took off her reading glasses, folded them carefully into their gunmetal case, and looked slowly up at Grace under her silver eyelashes.

'She's not well I'm afraid. You can leave her a message if you wish,' she continued dreamily. Grace then caught her eye. 'You're Simon's … stepdaughter, aren't you?'

'Yeah.'

'Could you ask the dear darling to give me a ring? There's a freelance art writer in town who's knocked over by his latest stuff. Dying to interview him, probably for something quite … glossy.'

'I don't know where he is at the moment.'

'Ah well. When you run into him do remember to ask.' She reached for her glasses again in dismissal, then added, 'I've left messages for him everywhere.'

'Yeah,' said Grace, 'I have too.' As she was leaving the shop she turned, 'Doesn't Jo know where he's gone?'

'Apparently not.'

'OK. Thanks.'

Grace went out into the street to join Stacey, who was gazing unseeingly into the window.

'Nobody knows where he is, Stace. I think we'd better go up to his studio. I've got a key to it.'

'OK,' said Stacey tonelessly. 'Do you want me to come?'

Grace squeezed her arm. 'Come on.'

They walked silently up the steep lanes of the town in the spring sunshine. When they reached the studio Stacey stayed outside while Grace went up the stairs. The studio was empty and familiar, but it felt wrong.

'Stace. Come up a minute. He's not here.'

Stacey came in and sat on a stool by the window. Grace went over to the winking answerphone and pressed the button. There were five or six messages for Simon, one from his agent and the rest from people Grace knew, all variations on the theme of 'Where are you?' She walked around, then stopped with a shock and said 'Look!' Stacey slipped heavily off the stool and came to see. An easel was lying on its back, and nearby was a completed abstract with a large ragged hole in it.

'Looks like he had a bit of a mental,' said Stacey.

'Shit ...' said Grace. 'That would have been worth loads of money. Whatever made him do that?'

'Maybe someone's broken in,' said Stacey.

Grace walked around through the slanting light, checking the windows. Stacey remained where she was, gazing down at a stain on the floor.

'Is that paint or blood?' she said flatly. Grace came over and squatted down to look. She went out to the toilet and came back with a damp tissue. She rubbed the marks, which spread pinkly through the tissue.

' 'S blood, isn't it?' said Stacey, who had seen blood on the floor too often.

'Yes,' said Grace, 'but nobody's broken in.'

'Perhaps he cut himself, when he lost it. Whatever it was it looks like he's run away.'

'Yeah,' said Grace. 'Bugger it. We can't ask him if we can borrow the flat if he's not here.'

Stacey didn't answer for a few moments. Then she shook her hair and said, 'Never mind. It was a nice thought.'

'We'll go anyway,' said Grace suddenly, nodding her head to emphasise her words. 'Mum'll get fed up with you being at home soon, and you can't go home. And you don't want to end up with Aunt Rosemary.'

'Fuck, no. She never helped Mum when she needed her.'

'Let's take some stuff around there now.'

Forty-five minutes later they were standing outside Simon's flat while Grace extracted another of her seemingly inexhaustible supply of secret keys. Each of them carried a rucksack and a full bin bag. They knocked before they went in, but the flat was empty too. For the first time Stacey became animated. She explored the cupboards eagerly and exclaimed at the contents of the fridge. She put her things around the bathroom and stretched out her sleeping-bag on the spare bed. She found the kettle and tea-things and busied herself around the kitchenette.

'Brilliant place for a party, Gracie,' she said.

'Better not. Not until he knows we're here anyway.'

The answerphone messages were much the same as in the studio. Plus one: 'Simon ... just to let you know ... I've decided to keep it ... I really need to talk to you ... er congratulations or something ... call me ... Bye ...'

Neither girl referred to it.

'Let's go and get some bread. We can make some toast,' said Stacey.

'Yeah,' said Grace, happy to stoke up her enthusiasm. She left a note on the table in case Simon turned up, and they went off to the shops.

Later Stacey gulped from one of Simon's beer cans and gazed down towards the harbour.

'He'll never find me here ...' she said, and Grace knew she meant Gary.

'No, he won't,' she replied. 'And if he did,' she added quietly,

'I'd kill him.'

'Simon's so good at drawing. And marvellous at watercolours. His teacher says he's never seen such a sense of colour in one so young. Simon, darling, go and get your painting-book out. The big one.'

Simon woke from his doze to the sound of his mother's voice. He stretched and flashed the torch for a second. His watch said daytime, but no light penetrated the shaft. So good at colours. Here there were none. His mother seemed reluctant to fade back into his dream. Such talent. Such promise. His sister had trudged through her growing up, ordinary, nearly monochrome against his luminous temperament. He had been chosen. He had climbed onto his talent like a board and begun to surf through life. The one-man show. The cat who walked by himself. And when things got tight he simply disappeared for awhile. A small case, a credit card, a passport. And after a suitable interval, back home to see how much he had been missed. Do artists have to explain? No, they do what they must. They are keepers of the flame, and beyond question.

He had tidied his space. He found some stones and pebbles, and spelled out Christopher James' name on his mound. He drank the earth-tasting water, and observed how his hunger grew. Sometimes he attacked the sides of his prison with the shovel, risking further roof falls. Sometimes he shouted and even screamed. It warmed him to do so, but each time he rested the cold seemed to seep further into his limbs.

This time the cat had found something it couldn't get out of. The pussy was in the well. And nobody knew it was there. Or cared. How long before he would be missed? Days? Perhaps weeks? He sucked on a smooth pebble for something to do until panic blazed up once more and he flew at the walls with his shovel.

Jo's mother came down to stay with her, a small shrewd woman with Jo's smile and love of straight talk, but less of her humour. They got on, but Jo kept catching her eyes upon her. It was a new look, not pity, a little like respect, and another emotion running even deeper. Jo didn't care to put a name to that, because it was somewhere in the general area of 'Now you'll see …' But they talked long into the night as they had never talked before.

Stacey and Grace burrowed deeply into Simon's flat. It was the perfect antidote to Stacey's grief, she never grew tired of the novelty of it. Grace could see her relaxing, perhaps for the first time ever.   They talked all about Brenda, but Stacey showed little pain. She was happy to eat, drink, talk, watch TV, and sleep, which she did for hours, mostly in the daytime. Grace remembered to worry about Simon when there was time, but she had grown up used to unexplained absences beyond her control.

Jane revelled in the space and peace for a couple of days. Then she got bored and invited a handful of friends to stay, long enough to give her cause to complain.

Andrew Statham worried on and off, nagging Jo, Ti, Jane and everyone he knew. Time was getting on, and he needed Simon there. The paintings were not enough. The media needed to be cranked up and only Simon could do that. He grew increasingly hoarse, but impossible artists were his life and he was slow to panic.

Days passed.

Simon tracked back through every girlfriend he had ever had, from Jo to his friend Richard's sister who kissed him at a party when he was nine. Her name had been slow to return, but he had it now. Anthea. He could feel her thin closed lips pressing on his. All his senses were dulled but it made his memories brighter, sometimes brighter than he could bear. He relived a long walk by a canal with Sue, the girl he had first brought to Cornwall. It was almost tangible in its clarity, the sound of the birds, a train which passed them, her warm hand in his. He watched the two of them every step of the way, then looked at his watch to find only a five minutes had passed. Another time he squatted down to remember his childhood bedroom, and found that two hours had passed. Time was slipping, and he knew that it was.

But time was all there was. Seeing out the time. He was not shouting any more, hardly using the dimming torch. Only when the panic attacks set in he would lunge around, sometimes in the pool itself, attacking all the walls in the dark often with his bare, bleeding hands, grunting like a bear, hearing earth falling here and there, not caring, hoping for a large fall which would put an end to time. But time would not let him go.

In a period of clear-headedness he walked again with Jane along a crystal-white beach. Was it Greece? Sicily? Scilly? He couldn't remember. They saw no-one else all afternoon. They lay on the sand and occasionally went in and out of the water, too happy even to talk, never wanting it to end. Jane sunbathed naked next to him, but lazily pushed him away until the red sun was falling into the sea. Then she reached out and pulled him over onto her sun-warmed body.

Was it after that? Soon after that, surely, he asked her to marry him. Jane, will you marry me? She had looked at him and laughed in frank astonishment. Why would I want to do that? She'd already been through that one, she explained. She'd done marriage, done childbirth, done motherhood. They were all overrated. All she wanted now was a good time.

He had laughed with her at his own absurdity. But things were never quite the same afterwards. He must have minded, although he had never said so or thought so before. He'd never been married, never offered a woman the gift of himself. He felt slighted. Passion turning to division, friction turning to battle. War and peace, and war again.

And then the last public Private View. Coming home to find the locks changed. Jane's voice on the phone telling him to disappear. Blood and wine on the carpet. A fascinated audience observing their last rites.

His mother's voice broke into his thoughts. She was the only constant in a world of occasional delusions, the voice most in his head, the theme of his nightmare, through the darkness, on and on: 'Come and see what Simon's done. What do you think of that? Look at those colours … Better clear up now before your father gets home. You know he hates a mess.'

24

'Jane ... I'm really sorry ...'

The voice on the other end was unrecognisable. 'What?' it said thickly.

'I'm sorry to disturb ...'

'Who is this?'

'It's Jo.'

'Joe? Who the hell's that? I don't know anyone called Joe in daytime, let alone at this time of night. You sound like a woman.'

'I am. It's just ...'

'Jo? As in 'Little Women'?' Are you that ... child that Simon's been seeing?'

Jo held her temper. 'Yes.'

'For Christ's sake.' A pause. 'Do you know what time it is?'

'Yes.'

'What d'you want?'

'Have you seen Simon?'

There was another pause. Jo imagined her opening her eyes properly, blinking away the wine, taking a deep breath ...

'Yes. Of course. He's right here. Right beside me.'

Her face was suddenly hot.

'He is?'

'Yes. I'd put you on to him, but he's tied to the bedposts and gagged with a silk scarf. No, of course he's not here. I threw him out months ago, remember? Into your lap.'

'He's ... missing.'

'How poignant. Good. That was worth waking up for. Did no-one tell you he doesn't usually stay with ladies for long these days?'

'He's been gone for nearly a fortnight. Nobody knows where he is.'

'Did you have words?'

She could hear Jane moving, sitting up in bed, making herself more comfortable.

'Do tell.'

'It's alright,' Jo said tonelessly. 'It was just a thought. I'll ring the police.'

'You can't do that,' rasped Jane, 'I was just starting to enjoy myself. So, when did he go?'

'Sorry to have woken you.'

Jo heard her growl, 'It was a pleasure,' as she lowered the phone. She wound the duvet more tightly around herself and went back to the sofa, with Jane's rich laughter in her ears.

Grace met Jo by chance in a queue at the supermarket. They discussed Simon's disappearance, each looking to the other for clues. Their worried conference continued on the pavement outside, but they parted without a conclusion. Then Grace went to the police. In a sterile room she spoke, after a long wait, to a kindly middle-aged WPC. How long had he been missing? Nearly a fortnight. Had he ever gone missing before? Yes, but not for a long time. Had Grace checked with his family? Yes as much as possible. Had he any relationships? Yes, he had a girlfriend. Grace added that she seemed to be pregnant, and the WPC smiled a wordly-wise smile. Grace lost her temper completely, and demanded that the police check whether his passport or his credit cards had been used; or put him on a missing list; or did something more than sit there laughing at her as if she was a stupid kid. The WPC calmed her down a little and sent her away. Grace went to Jane. Jane didn't want to be bothered about where Simon had hidden himself.

Grace screamed at her. She yelled back. Only when she heard that Grace had been patronised by the police did she swing into action, and sailed down to the police station like a yacht in a stiff wind.

Under her attack they promised to list him as missing, and carry out a few enquiries. But it was clear that they still thought it was a waste of time. At Grace's insistence they tested the blood on the studio floor, and later found that it was Simon's. But who else's should it have been? There were no signs of a break-in or a struggle, apart from the damaged painting. He'd cut himself, so what?

Slowly Simon's disappearance became public knowledge. A piece in the local paper was picked up by Andrew, now desperate, and amplified to the art press and later the national papers. Andrew had a couple of emergency conferences with his regular PR firm. If he could not have his artist in residence he would have to make something of his mysterious disappearance. It worked surprisingly well. Present artists giving voluble press copy on their latest exhibitions were commonplace, but an exhibition by a missing person was a new angle. There were even sightings in European resorts, and a few reporters came to Cornwall to ask questions and take photographs in between afternoons on the beach. They took pictures of his studio, reproduced some of his paintings, knocked on Jane's door until she swore at them, called on Ti who gave them polite interviews and elegant photographs of herself. One paper even resurrected pictures of Simon emerging from the earth. It was a trickle rather than a flood, and none of it brought Simon any closer to light. Buoyed up by mystery, the publicity for his exhibition grew and grew. He had made the break-through he longed for before he had even opened.

Jo avoided any encounters with the press, passing them all onto a grateful Ti. She had long believed that Simon was far away. Jo was sure her big mouth on the answerphone must have sent him running for cover. She would not be surprised to see him stay away for a year or so until the baby was born and the new regime was established, whatever it might be. Grace called in to see her almost every day, increasingly anxious. One day she looked at Jo with her small intense face and said, 'I know about the baby.'

'How?'

'Your message. I've wiped it now.'

Jo had started to like Grace, and trust her.

'Do you think that's why he went?' she asked.

Grace shook her head. 'I don't think he ever got the message. Most of his stuff was still in the flat. I don't think he left the country.'

'So where is he?'

'I just can't think. He's such a bastard. All he needs to do is ring.'

But later, in a quiet moment, Jo remembered again the excited tone of voice of Simon's last message, the sudden warmth in his voice as he apologised and promised her an explanation. A shapeless woman had broken down in front of one of his paintings. How could that be so exciting? Her mind had circled the subject so often there was nothing left to think.

She gave up, and turned her attention once more to the pregnancy magazine she was hiding on her lap. Her eye fell on a series of diagrams of foetal development, disturbing in its familiarity. Then she looked straight up to where a colour supplement photograph had been stuck on the wall, of *Painting No 5*.

Suddenly Jo knew. The painting wasn't an abstract, not even an evocation of an unborn child as some critics had suggested. The light bulb shape, the eye socket, the colour and proportions, were all too precise. That was what lay behind its shock value. It was no arty conundrum. It was real, a real skull, a real baby. Somewhere it existed in a real place. She spoke out loud to the painting.

'Where are you?'

Then her nails bit into her palms.
The mine.

'I've brought you your favourite. Scrambled eggs. See how yellow they are.'
Eggs.
Jo had eggs. Jane had eggs too, but she wouldn't share them. His chest was as cold as his father's when he had kissed his dead face.
'I hate eggs. They taste of shit.'
He missed the darkness. The flashing lights blinded him and wouldn't stop. The walls moved in and out as he breathed. He was inside a cold lung which wouldn't stop breathing. He could count the blood vessels in the walls, onetwothreesixtwelve. In. And then out. And again.

Was I ever upright? Did I stand? Only when women were there. A woman always a stick in hand, padded pad in armpit, spine-stiffener, penis too, so that I never fell, and so I never rose, not alone. Addict. Habit. Kill the beast.
'That's lovely, dear. What is it?'
'It's after a car crash with lots of bodies and blood and bits of insides, and rats having lunch in it, Mummy.'
'I'm still smiling Simon. You can't say anything which will make me stop.'

At least the last feeling had gone, from the nail-less fingers, the aching legs, the howling stomach. No voice left. I'm coming, Christopher.

'Don't throw your drink on the floor darling. People will think you're spoilt. I'll tell your father it was me. Look, Ribena, it makes a purple stain, you'll use that colour one day'
'Fuck off Mother, before I bite out your throat …'

'You're such a clever boy. Shall I fetch your paints? You can do a painting of my bitten out throat and show it to your teacher'

Is it time Chris? Jo's baby? Are we there yet? How many stops to go?

'I've brought you some orange juice …'

Too late. Look no hands. Nothing to pull my eyes out with …

25

Jo remembered to breathe, and broke into a sweat. The mine shaft, of course. And the woman. She had seen her there herself, standing in the dark keeping vigil, sowing little threads to the top of her child's grave. How could she not have seen it before? Why hadn't Simon said? He liked to skate away from involvement, but he'd finally found something he couldn't get his head around …
Jo felt dizzy and sick. She must ring Grace. Whose friend's mother had … oh Jesus.

'Jo, are you alright?' Richard had come into the gallery without her noticing. 'Don't want to be rude but you look quite awful. Heard you'd been poorly.'
'Could I just go out for some air?'
'Course. Gallery won't be busy on a fine day like this. I'll keep an eye.'
'Thanks.'

The street was quiet with just a few relaxed visitors, families chattering, unpressed by time. For a while Jo could not make herself move. Only her mind was racing, replaying every event in the weeks since Simon's fall against her new knowledge, every word and glance re-aligned to a different context. She lurched desperately from one line of thinking to another, trying to locate the one which led from there to here, the one which would tell her where on earth Simon could be. Finally she jerked into movement.

The blue flame was perfect, like a huge gas jet, cool and round and beautiful. It was blue all the way up, right up into the shaft. He lay contentedly beside it, watching Christopher breathe, occasionally stroking his fine hair. Somewhere behind him he could hear the distant sound of another baby's cry, and animals in the dark. Someone else could deal with that. It was quiet at long, long last. His eyes ranged up and down the flame, never tiring of its symmetry, up and down and round …

Stacey answered the door a crack, after a pause at the spyhole.

'Yeah?'

'Is Grace in?'

'No.'

'Is she coming back?'

'Who wants to know?'

'You're Stacey, aren't you?'

'Could be.' She focussed more closely on Jo's face, and Jo could see that she had been drinking.

'Can I come in?'

'Why?' said Stacey coldly, 'Who are you?'

'I'm Jo. Simon's girlfriend, remember?'

Stacey's face softened, and she opened the door. 'Come in,' she said. 'Sorry. My aunt's threatened to put the Social onto me. I thought you were one of them.' She closed the door carefully behind them.

The flat was very untidy, with clothes and cans and ashtrays and leftovers from takeaway meals scattered all over the sitting room. Jo looked around. She had not been here since Simon's cold dismissal a century ago. She wanted to cry, but that would have to wait.

'Stacey,' she began, 'you know Simon's missing …'

'Yeah, just a bit,' said Stacey. 'That's all Grace talks about. He's not even her dad …'

'I've found out a lot more about it.'

'You'd better tell Grace then. She'll be back in a minute.'

'I think it concerns you too.' Stacey stared at her angrily. 'And especially your mother.'

'My mum?' exploded Stacey. 'What's it got to do with her? She hardly knew Simon except as my teacher.'

'I know …'

'So what are you on about?' Stacey's eyes were red-rimmed and flicking with pain. 'I mean, like, she's dead you know. You did know that?'

'Yes,' said Jo, trying to keep herself under control. 'She died the same night that Simon disappeared.'

'What are you saying? That he killed her or something? You know that bastard Gary disappeared as well? That night? So what's going on?'

Grace had come in and stood uncertainly by the door.

'Yes, I've heard about Gary. I've been trying to put it all together in my mind, but I'm pretty sure now. Keep calm Stacey, please. I'll tell you what I think happened. You won't like it, but you need to know.'

Grace came and sat next to Stacey, but Stacey tossed her hair angrily and would not look at her.

'Go on,' she said dangerously.

Jo stumbled through her notion of what had happened, from when Simon first fell down the mine to Stacey's mother's visit to the gallery and Simon's excited pursuit. Stacey interrupted at first, then sat silently, gradually turning white.

'I think they must have met up,' said Jo, 'and after that I haven't any idea. Your mother died and Simon disappeared on the same night.'

'And Gary jumped ship,' said Grace quietly, 'so he must have known something.'

'Are you saying I had a brother, or a sister?' said Stacey in a dead voice.

'Yes,' said Jo.

'And my mum … and it ended up down a mine?'

Jo nodded.

There was a long pause. Grace got up silently and filled the kettle.

'That broken picture in the studio,' said Stacey suddenly, 'that would have been Gary. Typical. He did that.' She paused again. They sat in silence, trying to contemplate what calamity had exploded amongst them. Suddenly Stacey started to cry, softly like a small girl. 'Poor Mum,' she said. 'She's always been weird about babies. Real ones, even ones on the adverts. Never could look at one. That's why I …' But she broke off and wiped her eyes, allowing Grace to comfort her. There was another long silence.

'The mine …!' said Grace. The other two looked at her, but her eyes were closed.

'Simon would never have gone back there,' said Jo. 'Over his dead body …'

A deeper silence fell. They could hear the sound of daytime TV from the flat below.

Jo spoke, 'I'll get my car … '

Suddenly they were all moving.

Twenty minutes later they were driving over the moor, scattering the early afternoon rabbits into the gorse undergrowth. At the top they stopped and Jo ran to the head of the shaft.

'The wire's been cut …'

She wriggled between the cut barbed wire, and started to tug at the boarding. The other two helped her push over the heavy weights and pull a board aside until a corner of blackness appeared. They were sweating in the sun, working in silence. Jo shouted so loudly and suddenly that the other two jumped with fright.

'Simon!' she screamed into the hole, 'Simon!'

'Can you hear anything?' said Stacey.

'Be quiet! Simon! Can you hear me?'

She knelt down to listen. She remained kneeling for a while, calling again, while the others stood still. She listened again. Then she straightened up.

'Nothing,' she said.

'What shall we do?' said Stacey. Then she quietly said 'Oh, look!' They followed her downward gaze. On a rock amongst the debris within the barbed wire were two large candles, mostly burned away.

'Christ,' said Jo, her nausea returning with a rush.

Grace said, 'Get your mobile out, Stace. Call the police.'

Gradually under the early summer sunshine the moor began to fill up. Firstly came the police, then a cliff rescue team, an ambulance and two fire engines. They parked at odd angles at the side of the track, the vehicles shining in the bright light. The three women sat together on a bank, detached, saying as little as possible. A fireman gave them a cup of tea from a flask, which they shared. After a while another very grubby fireman appeared from the open wound in the ground. His face gave no message, and he went into a huddle with his chief and the police inspector. A policeman came over to them.

'There is someone down there. We're getting him out as soon as possible.'

'Is he dead?' said Jo, wondering at her own calm.

'We can't be sure at the moment. Sorry.' He turned to go back.

'Thank you,' said Jo.

'Officer?' said Stacey.

'Yes miss?'

'There might be another body down there.' The policeman looked at her uncomprehendingly. 'A baby. Been there a long time. Could you please look for that as well?'

He nodded slowly, then hurried back to the group of men. A

second ambulance was bumping up the lane to join them.

Simon's body, strapped firmly to an orange stretcher standing on end came up some time afterwards. And then a small black plastic bundle. The paramedics clustered around Simon's white mud-streaked face. Jo clutched hands with the others. Very quickly they loaded him into an ambulance and went off down the hill. The policeman came back, wiping his forehead.

'We're not absolutely sure. It doesn't look very good, to be honest. He's very cold.'

He stood up awkwardly. The women waited for more. He cleared his throat and said, 'Could someone tell us what they know about the other … the baby?'

They all stared ahead for a moment.

'We'll come,' said Grace at last, getting up. 'C'mon Stace. You'd better go straight to the hospital,' she added to Jo.

'I suppose I shouldn't be asking you this,' said the policeman, 'but you obviously know a lot more than I do. Are we looking at a Crime Scene here?'

'Yes,' said Grace.

'Two,' said Stacey.

26

The hospital became Jo's world for a while. Like a village she became familiar with its population and its noises and rhythms. Simon had died soon after his first admittance, but shocks and heat treatment had started his thin, stubborn pulse again. They had brought his body temperature up by slow degrees. The police came and looked at the bruises on his unconscious body, assessing which were caused by his attempts to escape and which had a different source.

Stacey and Grace came with clothes and supplies for Jo, and news. Brenda's body had been released for burial, and it had been agreed that the remains of the baby could lie beside her, once the facts detailing his brief existence had been documented. The police had attempted to interview the old man, but he had reacted with blank and sometimes violent incomprehension. Rosemary had refused to answer questions and since she was not under suspicion the police could not compel her. Attempts to locate Gary had been stepped up but there was no sign of him, and Stacey expected none.

Simon lay in a deep coma while the rota of nurses took care of him, feeding, cleaning, checking his respiration. He had started to breathe unaided, but the consultant explained carefully to Jo that no-one could be sure when he would recover consciousness, if he ever did, how much brain activity he had, whether irreparable brain damage had occurred, and if so how much, and more in that vein.

175

After a week she went back home, and visited the hospital every afternoon. Sometimes Grace came with her.

'What made you decide to keep the baby?' she asked one afternoon.

'I don't really know,' said Jo. 'I was surprised at myself to tell the truth. I'm quite OK about abortion. My friend Nadia was furious with me. She thinks I'm betraying womankind. But I'm not even doing it for Simon, I don't think.'

'Did – do you love him a lot?'

'Don't know that either. I really liked him, but I don't know if I ever knew him. If he came back to life and started being, you know, Simon again, I don't know how long it would last. There isn't much room for anyone else but him in his life.'

'No,' said Grace, 'I'm OK about abortion too. In spite of my mother telling me so often she wished she'd gone through with hers instead of having me.'

'Did she really say that?'

'Loads of times. She really meant it too.'

Jo stared at Grace's face which was calm and free of self-pity.

'On the other hand,' Grace went on, 'it saved Stace's bacon.'

'How?'

'She had an abortion in Year Nine. Don't tell her I told you.'

The door of Simon's room opened behind them. They looked up as Jane came quietly in.

'Sorry,' said Jane, self-conscious for once. 'I didn't realise you were both here.'

'Would you like to sit down?' said Jo, but Jane said, 'No, it's alright. I was just passing.' Jane looked at the figure in the bed for a while in silence, her face unreadable.

'Did you hear about the other, the baby?' she said finally in a small voice. 'One of the policemen I know told me.'

'Brenda's baby?' said Jo.

'No,' said Jane, her face suddenly devoid of vitality, showing its age. 'No. The other one. They really went through the place.

There was another one down there in the mud. Must have been there best part of a hundred years. And a couple of dogs,' she added

'God,' said Jo.

'I suppose a mineshaft's a bit like an attic, isn't it, where things get lost or hidden away. Keeps things tidy. Trust Simon to choose that one to fall into.' said Jane, with a ghost of a smile. 'Congratulations by the way.'

'Thank you.'

Jane stood lost in thought for a moment, seemingly about to speak and changing her mind. Jo said, 'I just can't understand why he didn't say something. If it was eating him up like that. Why didn't he tell …' she looked at the others ' … one of us?'

'They don't,' said Jane. Then she leaned over and kissed Simon gently on the forehead.

'Silly boy,' she said. She went straight for the door, waving to them with her fingers. 'Come and see me, Grace. Come and get a decent meal inside you. Byee.'

For a while neither of them could think of anything to say. Jo stared into space, seeing *Painting No 5*.

'Good old Jane,' said Grace. 'Nothing throws her for long.'

'She's missing you,' said Jo.

'Don't,' said Grace. 'I don't want to think about it.'

Eventually Jo said 'Getting back to your question, once it was happening – and I really didn't mean it to – I just didn't feel like stopping it. There never seemed to be a right time. It does sound drippy doesn't it? The only thing that really worries me now is how pleased my mum is. I thought she'd be furious. I think I've finally entered the sisterhood or something. What a terrible thought …'

They both laughed.

'Don't worry,' said Grace. 'Anyway I can see myself as an auntie. I'll buy a shawl.' Jo smiled at the idea. They sat in companionable silence. After a while Grace said, 'I'm going back to the flat now.'

'Is Stacey still there?'

'Yeah. But she's got a new boyfriend now, so she's mostly round at his.'

'OK. Look after each other.'

'You too.'

Jo was surprised to feel the touch of Grace's dry kiss on her cheek before she slipped quietly out of the room. She turned her attention once again to the study of Simon's eyes and eyelashes as they responded to waves of internal colours, washing up and down, round and round, never still, twitching and fluttering, seeking for equilibrium in an endless abstract dream.